The Invincible Will

Amadi Ekwutosilam Njoku

Ukiyoto Publishing

All global publishing rights are held by

Ukiyoto Publishing

Published in 2023

Content Copyright © Amadi Ekwutosilam Njoku

ISBN 9789360169367

All rights reserved.
No part of this publication may be reproduced, transmitted, or stored in a retrieval system, in any form by any means, electronic, mechanical, photocopying, recording or otherwise, without the prior permission of the publisher.

The moral rights of the author have been asserted.

This is a work of fiction. Names, characters, businesses, places, events, locales, and incidents are either the products of the author's imagination or used in a fictitious manner. Any resemblance to actual persons, living or dead, or actual events is purely coincidental.

This book is sold subject to the condition that it shall not by way of trade or otherwise, be lent, resold, hired out or otherwise circulated, without the publisher's prior consent, in any form of binding or cover other than that in which it is published.

www.ukiyoto.com

Dedication

To the evergreen memories of my most beautiful and affectionate mom, Glory Amadi Njoku (Nne Orieoma) and Ichie Amadi Njoku (Nna Charlie), Osuru oha ji; who was a total and great father.

Chinua Achebe, the maverick griot, who trailed the ancient path, not laurels denied.

Acknowledgments

To all members of the English Language Teachers Association of Nigeria (ELTAN) in Lagos State and all English teachers nationwide—my sincerest gratitude for championing national development through English.

Scott McCormick for reading my manuscript and returning it with honest feedback.

Professor Angel Davis for introducing me to great writings.

H.R.H Omezue Idam Onya Bassey, the Ubaghala 111 of Amasiri Autonomous Community, Honourable Obiageri Oko Enyim, Chairperson, Afikpo North Local Government, for living up to the mandates and lifting the banners of hope for your people.

Isoken Joy Imafidon for being so supportive.

I am unlikely to forget Anwuli Ojogwu, ED/Co-founder of Society for Book & Magazine Editors of Nigeria (SBMEN), and Eghosa Imasuen, author of Fine Boys, for introducing me to the world of editing and teaching me the ropes.

There are many others, though more than deserving of mention, whose names, for now, I would not disclose.

About the Book

Coming from a 'bush' school to join a city one, young Achebe is determined to let his teachers and friends know that no force can withstand a mind imbued with an invincible will to succeed. Not only does he attain his dreams, but he also gains fame so that even his traducer is forced to admire him.

Sometimes, the best stories are not the ones dealing with the unfathomable complexities of this life. Sometimes, the best stories are just simple didactic stories leaving us feeling nostalgic after reading them; this is what Amadi E. Njoku's *Invincible Will* represents to me as I leafed through its pages.

It is a novella worth reading and keeping for adults. And as for the younger generation, I am sure this story will be counted among the fond memories of childhood as you advance into adulthood.

Ubaji Isiaka Abubakar Eazy

Poet, Literary Critic, and Book Reviewer.

Contents

Achebe in Lagos	5
Achebe's First Day at School	7
Lotanna, the Entitled Brat	10
After School	12
Kay, the Bully	14
Achebe Comes Top in His Class	17
The Character of a Champion	20
Achebe Writes to Ugonna	22
Chapter Ten: The Book Eating Spirit	25
Chapter Eleven: The Announcement	30
Beans Myth	34
Leaving Adult Things for Adults	39
A Gift	43
The Fight	47
Achebe's Dream	50
Achebe Meets Segun	53
A Leap of Faith	56
The Games	62
Achebe Laughs the Longest	66
About the Author	71

Achebe Informs Ugonna of His Journey to Lagos

Achebe and Ugonna became best friends while they were in primary three. The duo attended a village school, Ozara Primary School, the first missionary school in Amasiri, their hometown. Achebe was always punctual to school but Ugonna was habitually late. His teachers always warned him about his perpetual lateness but he turned a deaf ear. One day, Ugonna had it the hard way. On his way to school, he fell into the hands of civil brigades whose duty, among other things, was to kick against indiscipline and discourage loitering of pupils and students outside their schools. The loitering culture was becoming a culture among the students. They had caught Ugonna at some distance from the school and one of the civil brigade men asked him to tug his ears and jog to school singing a song of promise never to be late to school again while his tormentor followed him behind.

Ugonna jogged to school singing thus:

Aga ghim abia late ozo oh – I will never come late again.

Aga ghim abia late ozo oh – I will never come late again.

Aga ghim abia late ozo oh – I will never come late again.

Nke mu mbiara abia oharim n'eze – I have suffered a great deal for coming late.

Okpukpu ntari ata oharim n'eze – The bone I have been eating is now stuck in my teeth.

When they had covered a short distance, Ugonna became very tired and was pleading with his punisher, promising that he would never be late to school again. He was breathing heavily, yet the man did not listen to him. He followed Ugonna to school and handed him over to his class teacher and asked his teacher to give him grass to cut. Ugonna's teacher gave him a blunt cutlass and showed him a portion of grass behind their class to cut as punishment for his habitual lateness. He made a few attempts at the grass and after a while, beads of sweat began to trickle out of his body. Then he broke down in tears, but their teacher insisted he must finish cutting the grass. While other pupils said such punishment served Ugonna right, it was Achebe who had pity on him and went to assist him when their teacher was out of sight.

Ugonna was very grateful that Achebe came to help him. He thanked him many times and promised to turn a new leaf. Achebe and Ugonna became best of friends ever after. They always studied together and shared their future dreams with each other. They had hoped to gain admission into the same secondary school and graduate from the same university even though they wished to pursue different careers in life. Ugonna once told Achebe that he envied his fluency in English Language, his spirit of not quitting as well as his persuasive skills and would love him to build a career as a politician. But Achebe passed his hand twice over his head as if to reverse a curse and said he forbade such career in Jesus' name. He said politicians were dishonest people who never keep their promises. He wanted to become a great athlete, a sprinter.

But that was three years ago. Now the duo alongside other primary six pupils were due to sit for their National Common Entrance Examination for admission into Junior Secondary School (JSS 1) of the Federal Government Unity Colleges in Nigeria. Before 9 a.m. on that fateful day, Ozara Primary School was filled with pupils from other schools who had also come to sit for the same examination. The pupils of Ozara Primary School wore white and blue uniforms. It was common to see pupils' shorts - especially the rough and playful ones - bearing numerous patches of different shapes and sizes. Ugonna's pair of shorts had king-sized patches with multiple colours and they gave him an easily-recognised appearance from any distance. Without any thoughts of decency, the last Obioma (nomadic tailor), had woven and interwoven pink threads on old green and yellow ones. People preferred them because their services were cheaper compared to the conventional tailors. It didn't take Achebe long to spot his friend from the rest of the crowd that had gathered under the gmelina trees that provided shade for food and snacks' vendors behind the primary five classroom block. Ugonna had bent over to make his choice of biscuits from the assortment contained in different cartons when Achebe walked towards him.

"I knew you would be here," said Achebe as he clasped Ugonna on the shoulder.

"Yes, I just needed to eat something before the exam starts," replied Ugonna.

"So you cannot fast the whole day?" teased Achebe.

"You know that's not possible," said his friend.

When Ugonna had made his choice, he raised his head and folded his arms with his palm full of biscuits and waited for Achebe to buy his. They both strolled leisurely around the school premises, eating their lunch of biscuits, conversing.

"I'm happy today is going to be my last day in this school. Once we're through with the exam, what else? Final goodbye of course! I can't wait to be a student of Government College, Afikpo, by next session," Ugonna finished with an air of optimism.

"Me too," Achebe struggled to speak with a mouthful of biscuits. "I would have been happier than you if I were to go to Government College as I had chosen. But unfortunately, I won't be schooling anywhere in the East."

"Why? What happened?" Ugonna halted and folded his arms as he leaned against a gmelina tree and listened as Achebe tried to sit at its base before he said anything else.

"My uncle came in from Lagos yesterday. He said I would be travelling to Lagos with him after my common entrance exam. He also said that I would be schooling there."

"Though that's a good idea, I feel sad that we're going to be away from each other soon. Lagos is such a beautiful city my dad once told me," said Ugonna in a broken voice.

"I know. I'm going to miss you so much. If my opinion counted, I would say no to my uncle and stay back in the village. But my mother had warned me against such protest."

"I'll miss you as well. I hope you write to tell me many things about Lagos and your high school," said Ugonna as he looked away from his friend to conceal the little tears rolling down his cheeks.

"I'll write to you as soon as I can," Achebe promised as he rose to embrace him tearfully.

Achebe in Lagos

Achebe travelled with his uncle to Lagos a day after his National Common Entrance Examination. It was a long and tiring journey from Amasiri to Lagos especially for Achebe. Unlike his uncle who was already used to the distance, it was Achebe's first time to embark on such a long journey. As soon as they arrived, Achebe saw for himself that Lagos is a beautiful city just as Ugonna's father had told him it was. He saw that it's not only beautiful, but also a big city. But what was strange to him at first was the deafening noise pollution largely from religious houses, automobiles and low cost generators popularly known as *I better pass my neighbour*, used among Nigeria's middle class population. Soon, he became used to it. Achebe had never travelled out of his village before. He knew he would miss his mother greatly, his younger sister, Julie, and his friend Ugonna whom he was very fond of, but the desire to travel to big cities like Lagos overwhelmed him. He was now thirteen years old, but it was strange to see that he was way shorter than other kids of his age.

Two months later, the results of the National Common Entrance Examination were released. Achebe was among the pupils on list A; meaning that he was qualified to be admitted into a Federal Government College, Afikpo. His uncle told him that his mother had phoned him earlier that day to inform him that he and his friend, Ugonna had passed. Achebe could not contain his joy when his uncle broke the news to him. His eyes brightened and his face broke into a wide smile.

Achebe's uncle was a washer man in Lagos; he lived in a rented one room apartment. He was not performing at a level lower than should be expected as he was already building a duplex in his village at thirty-two though yet unmarried. He never liked sending money down to the village for the building project. He knew of cases where city dwellers, after labouring hard to earn money, would send funds to their relatives in the hope that they would help to supervise their building projects at home only to find out later that such relatives squandered the money or used it to fund their personal projects. He never wanted to hear such stories that would leave one heartbroken. Thus, Achebe's uncle would always travel to the village himself to be sure that works were going on at the building site and ensure workers did not waste the estimated blocks and cement. He would then return to Lagos as soon the money he had budgeted for the project at a time had finished. He was Achebe's maternal uncle. As a laundry man, he had many clients to whom he provided dry cleaning and delivery services. He had a worker called Deji, an eighteen-year-old boy who came under his employment three months ago after he had written both his Senior School Certificate Examination (SSCE) and Unified Tertiary Matriculation Examination (UTME), pending when he would be offered a provisional admission into a university. Achebe's uncle was not a strict man; he was very free with people but had no friends. He said friends in his day are people who would desert you when the chips are down. He had agreed to take Achebe with him so the lad would help him do some house chores appropriate for his age such as washing of plates, sweeping the floor etc. before leaving for school while he himself was away from home.

"Congrats to you on your success," said Achebe's uncle, offering to shake hands with him. Achebe felt proud of himself, he was certain that he was going to pass. Happily, he extended his hand to his uncle and thanked him.

"That's alright. More wins." His uncle prayed. "Your mom said you have never taken second position in class all through your primary school. Keep the zeal burning even as you enter secondary school."

Achebe had merely affirmed his uncle's words with a gentle nod. He was a modest lad. How he had wished his uncle knew how extremely shy he felt with praise. "You'll start school next term. Just a few weeks from now. There are good public schools here in Lagos. I'll enroll you in one," his uncle said.

Achebe was excited when his uncle said those words. He could not wait to be in secondary school. As he sat completely engrossed in the TV that evening, he began to imagine how big and beautiful his high school would look like.

Achebe's First Day at School

Sasa Community High School, Sasa, was a well-known school in the area. It had magnificent buildings with a large compound adorned with beautiful flowers. The assembly ground was an open space just in front of the admin office with an elevated podium painted in green and white. Because it was the first day of resumption, some students had not resumed. However, a sea of students had filed themselves according to their classes on the assembly ground. Achebe's uncle had accompanied him to school that day. As was always the case, parents of new intakes waited patiently around the school compound for the assembly to be over so they could formalise their children's or wards' registration.

Mrs. Okolo conducted the assembly from the beginning. While other teachers dressed in their best outfits, she wore a blue pinafore that befitted her large size on top of a blue striped shirt like every other student and stood on the podium. The idea was to make the students—both old and new—feel at home and to see their teachers not as superiors but as friends. At first, the new students thought she was some kind of clown and they all struggled to suppress their laughter.

"Good morning, students!" Mrs Okolo greeted.

"Good morning, Mrs. Okolo," chorused the students.

"I have the honour," she continued, "to welcome you all back to school for the new academic year. I want to specially welcome the new intakes, the JSS 1 students to Sasa Community High School. To all those who sailed through their last promotional exams, my biggest congratulations. Of course the term has begun with a renewed vigour and the challenge ahead is great."

Mrs. Okolo continued her speech by advising and encouraging the students – they listened with rapt attention. Afterwards, the students marched into their respective classes. After Achebe had been enrolled and was shown the way to JSS 1A, he went straight to his class. A few minutes later, his class teacher, Mr. Olurebi William, said it was time they introduced themselves. He walked to the marker board and wrote: name, age, home address, primary school finished from and future ambition. He then asked the students to follow that order. The first student got up quickly and said he was Suleiman Lawal, he was eleven years old and he lived at No. 18, Darasimi Street. He finished from De-Citadel of Faith Primary School, and wanted to be a pilot. Mr. Olurebi William was very impressed by the boy's confidence and said: "That's great! You're welcome to Junior Secondary 1. You may now sit down."

"Next!" Mr. Olurebi would say after each student had said theirs in that order, mentioning big schools as well as their lofty future ambitions. All who had introduced themselves had had their primary education in Lagos. As the process went on, Achebe became nervous and restless. He felt timid as he niggled at the thought of his own age and primary school's name. Achebe was the next after Akin Lotanna.

"Yes, it's your turn," Mr. Olurebi said, pointing at Achebe. Suddenly, Achebe's face turned pale and his skin was covered with goose pimples. His initial excitement had become clouded by anxiety, and his heart was beating faster than normal. Slowly he said: "My name is Onuwa Achebe. I'm thirteen years old and I live at No. 10, Bammeke street. I finished from Ozara Primary School and I want to be a sprinter in the future."

Hardly had Achebe told the class what he wanted to become, when Lotanna said, ridiculing him, "I have never seen a short sprinter in my life before o." The whole class burst into an uncontrollable laughter except his teacher and Suleiman Lawal.

"Where is Ozara Primary School?" asked Mr. Olurebi, when the noise had died down. "In our village." Achebe became nervous in a crowd of strangers who merely laughed off his future ambition, as though he had just made a rib-cracking joke. After the introduction, the students settled down and began to copy the new term timetable written on the board.

All through the day, Achebe felt very sad and timid. He was not only way shorter than all of his mates but also two years older than some and three years older than most. During break, Suleiman Lawal approached him and told him never to be discouraged that he could become whatever he wanted to be despite his height. Although Achebe was a bright student and a good sprinter, he knew height was his major challenge. He used to be the second-fastest sprinter in Ozara Primary School during their Inter-House Sports Competitions. Nduka Eze always outran him. Lawal's kind words soothed Achebe and they became quick friends.

Lotanna, the Entitled Brat

Later that day Mr. Olurebi had called Lotanna and told him that it was wrong to mock someone because they were disadvantaged. In the end, he had told Lotanna to go and apologise to Achebe. Lotanna had only said he would in his presence but never did. He had said to himself that he would never stoop low to say he was sorry to Achebe. Pride was one of Lotanna's bad habits that he had picked up early in life. He had an excessive sense of his own importance.

Lotanna was a sooner child. He was conceived before his parents had wedded and was born afterwards. Though his mother was Igbo, his father, Mr. Akin, was a Yoruba man who had died after a protracted illness, leaving behind a great wealth for his family. Lotanna was only two years old then and he grew up having his wishes instantly gratified beyond the age where it was appropriate that he soon developed into an entitled brat. Because he was her only child, Lotanna's mother felt it was always right to provide him with whatever he wanted at his asking. Whenever she said no to his peremptory demands, Lotanna would sulk over the refusal and would not eat any food until such wish was met.

In school, he became mischievous and intolerant of other children. One day, his teacher had spanked him mildly for upturning a table in a rage that it hit a fellow pupil on the leg and injured him. The pupil had mistakenly dropped his backpack while attempting to hang his on the wall. Lotanna's teacher had rebuked him and told him that he was wrong to have injured a fellow pupil who had dropped his bag in error by acting violently. Lotanna was not remorseful. Rather, he threatened that he was going to report the teacher to his mother. The following day, Lotanna's mother stormed the school and was raging and shouting that all wondered if it was wrong to correct a child's negative behaviour.

"How dare you spank my child for reacting to damage done to his belonging like he is a thief, huh? If you're looking for whom to unleash your frustrations on in the name of discipline, it must not be my child okay," quarrelled Lotanna's mother as she pulled her son's teacher by the shirt, shaking.

"But no damage was done to his bag. Besides, I had only cautioned him for injuring his classmate on the leg," defended the teacher.

"Your duty is to teach and not to hit pupils under your care for whatever reason."

It took the prompt response of police officers whom the school's proprietress had contacted to quell Lotanna's mother's disgraceful act. That was how Lotanna's mother withdrew him from Great Leaders Primary School and enrolled him in another. Lotanna was a mommy's boy and she had babied him since birth that he thought everything he did was right, and others were wrong. He was not responsible for his own actions. Consequently, Lotanna became footloose and fancy-free.

After School

Achebe got home before his uncle. By the time his uncle returned around 9 p.m. that day, he had busied himself trying to draft his personal reading timetable. Achebe greeted his uncle and engrossed himself completely in what he was doing.

"How are you?" asked Achebe's uncle as he grabbed the remote control from the tempered glass centre table and switched on the TV before sitting down.

"Fine, uncle."

"Hope you like your high school!" said his uncle.

"Hmm...Yes! But..but-" Achebe muttered, his lips trembling.

"But what?" asked his uncle.

"Most of my classmates made fun of me when I told them what I wanted to become in the future. They laughed at me and said I was too short and even the oldest in the class," said Achebe. His uncle leaned back in his chair, cleared his throat and asked:

"Are there many students like you in school?"

"No." Achebe's response was a weak one.

"You're unique if that's so. It's normal for them to laugh at you."

"Unique? How do you mean, uncle? Achebe asked. Achebe was not hearing the word

for the first time but he wanted to know why his uncle had said so.

"It only goes to say you're special. There can be no other you anywhere. However, always stay away from those who think nothing good of you and get closer to those who believe in you and are proud of your individuality," he told Achebe. Those uplifting words from an uncle who saw good in all and was proud of one's individuality gave Achebe a gust of confidence and self-esteem.

"As you keep these in mind," he added, "you also have to prove to them that your brain is far taller than theirs."

"How do I do that, uncle?" asked Achebe, curious.

"Good. You should always stay at the top of the class. With that, they'll have to respect and not laugh at you anymore."

Achebe knew that to be at the top of his class was not as easy as his uncle had sounded but he was determined to come out on top if that could make others respect him. "Most of my mates attended big primary schools and may have been well exposed to learning," he said to himself. Achebe decided to put his shoulder to the wheel.

Kay, the Bully

A few weeks later, Achebe began to make new friends in school and Lawal became his best companion. He became more socially active and popular not only in class but also in the whole school. But he never allowed the spirit of popularity to keep him away from his studies. His personal time-table was the inner voice he always obeyed.

Achebe's class was always noisy any time there was no teacher in it, and sometimes too, the whole school would be thrown into a bedlam of noise as though it were a market place. But once there was a relative calm and he was free, Achebe would go to the school library to study. Sometimes too, he would use the school hall. One day, Achebe slunk out of his class to the library. With his Social Studies textbook tightly clutched to his side, he had barely walked past the walnut trees that lined themselves up along senior blocks when a loud voice bellowed at him.

"Hey! Stop there, small devil," said the unknown voice. But Achebe disregarded the voice and walked towards the library block, looking at every direction to see the caller. It was Kelvin, popularly known as Kay. He was fifteen years old and was in Senior High School Two (SHS 2). He always bullied junior students especially those who dared come anywhere near the senior blocks. He was a rebel; most students dreaded him like a disease and no teacher ever interfered with matters that involved him. Although Kelvin was a good athlete who had represented the school in various sporting events, he was a bone on the school's side.

Four years ago, Kelvin's father, Mr. Ajibade, had brought him back to Nigeria from the US. He was born in the US, thus, he was already growing up into a teen that wielded enormous powers than his parents. His parents had become too afraid to correct him whenever he did anything wrong for fear of being sent to jail. Because the laws of land overly protect children, Kelvin would tell his parents that he would call the cops for them if they ever beat him for any reason. But his father was never impelled to bring him to Nigeria—where he believed his son would be guided accordingly—until he had, one day, pulled a gun at him. How he wasn't shot at last only affirmed that his Chi was with him and did not want him dead yet. Soon after, Kelvin's father thought of what to do to prove to him that he was the one who had given birth to him and therefore, was wiser than he. During one summer holiday, Kelvin's father had lied to him that he wanted to take him to Nigeria, their ancestral land, for a two-week tour, and then return with him to the states. Kelvin who was unsuspecting became excited at the news about the trip. When they had arrived in Nigeria, Kelvin was enrolled in Sasa Community High School, a week later. His father had said he would continue schooling in Nigeria while living with an uncle until he had turned a new leaf. That, however, did not change Kelvin as he became even more delinquent in school and at home. He always talked back at teachers and said he could have shot them had he been allowed to come to Nigeria with his Glock, a handgun, cupping his fists in anger.

"You're deaf, right? Abi you no dey hear again?" Kelvin blurted out. His English was fine and still rhotic even when he struggled to speak disjointed Pidgin. Achebe had stopped, fearing, as Kelvin was now closing in on him.

"I heard you but my name is not small devil," Achebe said, trembling.

"Are you big? Ehn? Okay, big devil, have we not said that no junior students must pass through the senior blocks again?" said Kelvin as he gestured with a tug of his right ear.

"But I was only going to the library."

"It doesn't matter. You can even go to the White House if you like. My own is that you have gone against our rule. Kneel down fast," Kelvin commanded. Achebe had hardly said he was sorry and that he would not pass through the senior blocks next time when he got a hard smack. His plea, it seemed, had fallen on a duck's back and slipped away immediately.

"There's no next time in my vocabulary, you brat. I'm sure you will learn how to keep rules after dealing with you today," said Kelvin as he continued to bully his victim.

When Achebe told his friend Lawal about his ugly experience in the hands of Kelvin and said he wanted to report the matter to the school authority, Lawal advised him, as a good friend would, to lay the matter to rest. He told him that he would be in Kelvin's bad book if he found out that he reported him to anyone. Lawal also told Achebe that his elder brother who was in Junior High School Three (JHS 3) had once been bullied by Kelvin but got the worst from him because he reported him to the principal who threatened to suspend him from school for two weeks if he ever cowed any junior student again. But that did not stop him. If that happened, he would always come back for his victim after suspension.

"The fear of Kelvin is the beginning of wisdom," said Lawal. Achebe listened to his friend and resolved it was best to suffer once from his enemy than remain a perpetual victim. He was afraid that Kelvin would come for him again if he dared to report him to the school authority.

When Achebe got home that day he wanted to tell his uncle how he was bullied in school by a senior student but lacked the courage. Inasmuch as he knew that his uncle did not condone any act of disobedience—as he would even want to give a worse punishment for it—he also had his fears. Gallantly, Achebe resolved to bear the pain of his experience in silence.

Achebe Comes Top in His Class

By the eleventh week of the term, students had already written their exams. They anxiously waited for their results the following week. As teachers busied themselves in the staff room preparing results, some students were roaming around the school compound while others gathered in small groups, chit-chatting. Some boys also clustered themselves in the field to play monkey post—a Nigerian variation of five-a-side football. The monkey post game is played with a de facto ball known as *Health 5*, designed with black pentagons and a striking *5* font. It is made from rubber and wool and can take a good hit without swerving all over the place. Aside from being a means of relaxation and sweating out stress, it created some sort of social bonding and eliminated class differences among the students. The juniors were seen freely hobnobbing with their seniors, forming sets by picking from among themselves. Makeshift posts had been fixed using tyres and foot counts to ensure that both posts were of equal length. Four sets had been formed and Kelvin was among the first set that opened the match. Since there were usually no goalkeepers in the game of monkey post, Kelvin's set had chosen him to tend the goalpost by blocking shots with his feet and not his hands as well scare the opponents away with his muscular body.

It started slowly with accurate passes and impressive dribbles until it became fast-paced. All the players were good at the game, but it was John who seemed to have stolen the show. He was a skilled and better player, and he was playing against Kelvin's set. The students and the other sets who stood watching and waiting their turn applauded him to the echo with ayyyy, aaahhh! as he magically played 'snakebite' and 'leg over' tricks on his opponents, dribbling pass them and made straight to the goalpost. It would be the last goal that would knock his opponents off, but many believed Kelvin would intercept him! Could there be a right moment for him to attack? Quickly Kelvin launched himself forward like a dynamite to dispossess John of the ball. But he was in for a great shock. John had anticipated his next move and tactically faked him out as much as possible. He looped one foot over and around the ball, then pushed it away with the other foot as Kelvin drew closer and accelerated past him with a quick change of speed. It was too late for Kelvin when he tried to hinder him by dragging his hand, but his opponent was as slippery as an eel fish; instead, he came crashing waaaaah on the ground. And peeaam, he fired the ball into the goalpost. "GOAL OOO!" the spectators cheered joyfully. For a few moments, Kelvin buried his face on the ground in shame.

Achebe and his friend, Lawal, who sat at the feet of a walnut tree that stood beside the school hall watching and cheering John on, burst out laughing hysterically. Achebe seemed to laugh longer because it was an epic fall of an enemy and he liked it. He could not contain his joy and he was enjoying the game. Football was not his thing and he was not good at it, though he liked watching it. He was a great runner and a big fan of relay races. When he saw two students trying to outrun each other playfully from one end of the field to another the previous day, he remembered how he used to represent his primary school in relays and wished that his high school would organise such sport.

The Friday of the following week which marked the last day of the term was a day of anxiety for the students because they would be given their results. Though it was not a promotional examination, they knew that their performance in it would make or mar their chances of being promoted to a new class come third term. They had been told that they would be promoted based on their annual scores when the three terms' results were combined and divided by three.

The students had lined up in their respective classes for their results. At first, Achebe thought the results would be openly announced before everyone as was the case in the village schools so he became frozen with fear. He moved close to where he could hear the names as they would be called out by the teacher. There were occasions where the teacher's voice would be drowned by the murmurings of students who could not bury their anxiety as they would gather in an open space and listened to their teacher call out the names.

In such a method of announcing results, the teacher usually did not go through the rigour of reeling out the names of students who had failed. Only those who had passed would be called and those who did not hear their names knew they had failed. It was as simple as that. But that was the case in village schools some many many years ago. In contrast,

Achebe realised that each student was given a result sheet whether they passed or not. With that, one could choose to disclose his position to a classmate or keep it a secret. Whether then or now, everyone wants to be identified as a success and those who passed would leap for joy. Lawal had collected his result sheet before Achebe and he jumped up joyfully when he had glanced over it and saw that he had passed.

Most of Achebe's mates had predicted that it was Akin Lotanna who would come first. Only a few of them were not in that bandwagon. Lotanna, too, was cocksure about it that when he got his result, he quickly opened it. Lo, and behold! He was second. At that instant, he thought of his mother; he knew his mother would be displeased with him for not coming first. His face dropped in sadness and his curiosity mounted. He wanted to know who it was that had beaten him to the first position. A few other students had collected before it got to Achebe's turn. His anxiety had risen, too. But whatever position that awaited him, had he not worked hard for it? When he had received his, he swiftly checked his position before checking his grades per subject.

"Yes, I made it!" he blurted out. He had said this by closing his right fist and throwing it to the sky. Achebe was too thrilled for words. Other students were surprised to see that it was Achebe who had come top in his class except for Lawal. Lawal had always believed in his friend and was not in the least surprised that he came first. Lotanna was more surprised. He knew that the competition in his class was stiff and had burned the midnight oil to stay atop. He also knew that anyone else could beat him to the first position, certainly not Achebe who he had despised and called the ugly, stupid short boy from a primitive village.

That day Achebe could not wait to show his uncle his result. His joy knew no bounds. He ran home very quickly and soon found himself at No. 10 Bammeke Street where he lived.

The Character of a Champion

It was a quarter to three when Achebe got home. He knew that his uncle would still be at his laundry shop by that time so he quickly dropped his school bag. He took his result with him and zoomed off to his uncle's shop. Achebe never went to his uncle's shop unless on some Saturdays when he would be bored at home and wanted someone to talk to. So It was Deji, his uncle's worker, who saw him first from afar on this unusual day when he had left home to come to the shop. He was the one who told Mr. Okechukwu that his nephew was coming.

"Oga!" he said, "see as your little nephew is running excitedly to the shop like someone who has won an American Lottery." Achebe's uncle looked outside and saw that it was true and said in a way that showed he would have been more than happy if someone in his family had won the American Lottery too: "No one spits out honey that is dropped into his mouth. I wish he has won the American Lottery. What I have been so unlucky to win for six years now!" They had solely joked and laughed about that, though they knew that Achebe was still underage and so was not eligible to apply for the Green Card Lottery.

Achebe greeted his uncle and Deji as soon as he got to the shop and saw both of them laughing lightly at nothing in particular.

"This one that you came to shop today, hope all is well," Deji joked.

"Yes, brother Deji. There's no problem. I just want to show my results to my uncle," said Achebe, giving his uncle the creamy white result sheet. Achebe's uncle took a cursory look at his result; he felt very happy when he saw his position: "First out of fifty. That's great!" Then, he spent some time going through the subjects' grades. After which he praised Achebe for his outstanding performance but told him that he needed to improve on his Mathematics. Deji had also commended Achebe, telling him to keep it up. Next, Achebe's uncle's folded the result and dropped it inside one of the drawers in his shop.

Later that day while they were still in his shop, Mr. Okechukwu sat Achebe down and told him he wanted to have a word with him. First, he told Achebe that he was proud of him because he had done well, and wanted him to remain consistent if he ever wished to become a champion.

"You've done well no doubt by proving to those who mocked your height that you possess a taller brain than they," he said. Achebe felt proud of himself, his face glistening with a smile. "However," he continued, "success of any kind has its disadvantages, too. Like wealth, it requires discipline and consistency to build and maintain. It is better not to pursue it at all than to achieve it and let it fizzle out. What I'm saying is that as you have come top in your class this term, always strive to be first in class and in all you do, and that's consistency. It's the true character of a champion." Achebe was drawn in by the wisdom in his uncle's words that he nodded repeatedly like an agama.

Then he told Achebe that he would be travelling home during the weekend to roof his building and return in a week's time. Achebe was somewhat excited when his uncle told him this—it was, at least, an opportunity for him to write to Ugonna as he promised him he would even though he thought of how bored and lonely he would feel when his uncle was gone. But his uncle told him that he could always visit Deji at the shop whenever he was bored at home.

Achebe Writes to Ugonna

Achebe's uncle closed earlier than usual that day because he had to pack his luggage and get ready for the journey to Amasiri the following day. In the night after they had eaten their dinner of eba and oha soup, Achebe began to write the letter he wanted to send to Ugonna through his uncle. There was a blackout that night so they used a rechargeable lamp. Achebe lifted the lamp from the wall where it was hanging in order that it could evenly illuminate the room to the centre table where he had dumped his school bag before rushing out to his uncle's shop earlier that day. He unzipped his school bag and dipped his left hand into it. He brought out one of his exercise books and quickly tore out a piece of paper from the middle. He drew the plastic chair his uncle had bought for him for reading closer to the table and when he had written his address; he began:

Dear Ugonna,

I hope this letter finds you in good health. How're you and your studies at Federal Government College, Afikpo? I was so excited that you also made it to your dream college when the results of the National Common Entrance Examination were released. I have truly missed you and everyone else at home. However, I'm writing to tell you a lot of things about Lagos and my high school.

First, Lagos is truly a big and beautiful city as your dad had told you. It's a city that is thickly populated with people from different parts of the country and around the world. There are lots of beautiful houses with varying sizes. In the night, what you can see are sparkling lights from various houses, traffic lights, vehicle lights and street lamps, not stars and moon in the sky as we see them in Amasiri. However, there are lots of noise pollution from cars, industrial machines, and small generators popularly known as "I better pass my neighbour" used by most people, unlike the village that is calm and healthy.

Also, you might be surprised to hear that everyone in Lagos is a stranger even those living under the same roof. You hardly know who your neighbour is, whether he/she is a thief or a ritualist. There is a story of a young lady who was said to have splashed muddy water on a man with her car and drove off without saying sorry to him. The man who was dressed up for a job interview, looked at himself and saw how messy he had become and began to rain curses on the driver for being so wicked to him. Later that day, the man saw the same car that had soiled his dress parked outside the gate of the building he lived. When he had asked whom the owner was and explained how a young lady who drove it earlier had recklessly splashed muddy water on him without stopping to see the damage she had caused, he was told that the car belonged to one of his neighbours who had packed in about two weeks ago and that the young lady who had driven it was the neighbour's daughter. You see how people living in the same building could be strangers to themselves? In the village, you know virtually everybody and the bond is usually closer. Life in the village can be very physical. Every activity in the village requires physical exercise. For instance, one could work on the farmland, sow seeds into it, collect firewood for cooking, walk along old path leading to the stream, and do laundry himself. But in Lagos, most activities are done by machines. My uncle even has the one they call washing machine that does his laundry services for him and we use gas cooker for cooking. A neighbour has what is called a stationary bike. He uses it to exercise indoors as an alternative for outdoor biking.

The name of my high school is Sasa Community High School. It's a very big school with large and beautiful buildings. Its population is three times that of Ozara Primary School. Our uniform is blue striped shirt worn on top of navy blue shorts. The name of my class teacher is Mr. Olurebi William. I have few friends and one best friend whose name is Suleiman Lawal. His parents are from the north and he believes in me and my future dream of becoming a great sprinter when other students laughed at me and said I'm too short for that kind of dream. Guess what? I came first in my class and that surprised everyone.

    I'm excited at the thought of hearing from you soon. I have to tell you about a lot of things and expect the same from you. Send my regards to your mom and dad.

    Yours sincerely,

Achebe.

When Achebe finished writing the letter, he folded it and inserted it into a white envelope. He sealed it with his saliva by merely running his tongue over the inner edge of the flap of the envelope. Then he gave the letter to his uncle who was struggling hard to zip his overloaded travelling bag and told him it was for his friend, Ugonna, before going to bed.

****

Achebe's uncle spent two weeks in the village before returning to Lagos. He told Achebe how happy Ugonna was when he received the letter and promised he was going to write him back which he did. In his letter, Ugonna said that he was a boarder in Federal Government College, Afikpo, because his hometown was far away from school; that the secondary school is interesting, though it has its own challenges. He said that being outside the wings of his parents made him stronger and independent and that he had learned to work with time: he knew when it was time to play and when it was time to study. He went further to say that life in the hostel was not easy because there were lots of distractions and many times, he would want to read but feel discouraged either because he was tired or he had something else to do like taking care of himself, washing of clothes, or things that might be assigned to him by the head of the hostel. He also said that every Friday, his school organised sporting activities for students to participate in, that he enjoyed playing table tennis, volleyball and badminton. He also said that their school Inter-house Sports Competitions would come up the following term. Achebe was so excited to read his friend's letter and his voice resonated with him as he was reading it.

Chapter Ten: The Book Eating Spirit

Three weeks later, schools resumed and students were back to school. For many, it was an exciting experience, but it was a sort of mixed experience for Achebe. His friends welcomed him back to their fold and they were all glad to see each other again. Lawal told them how he had been longing for school to resume, reiterating that he was tired of running errands at home. This threw everyone into a laugher and Dapo called him a lazybone in Yoruba.

However, the air was filled with animosity and hate against Achebe and he could even smell them everywhere he went as he tried to get himself settled down for the term's works. He had become a bone stuck in the throats of those who felt he shouldn't have come first in the class and they never failed to show how much they hated him. But Achebe tried not to be overwhelmed by their hatred against him and moved on with his friends as though nothing bothered him. When others tried to be discreet with their dislike for Achebe, Akin Lotanna openly flaunted his hatred against him. He even hated himself more because his mother had scolded him for allowing a boy from a bush school to beat him in class.

Lotanna had a rapid growth that made him taller and bigger than most of his classmates. He had celebrated his tenth birthday a month before his admission into high school. He exhibited advanced skills and aptitudes at an abnormally early age. At four, Lotanna had already begun to read the newspaper. Because of that, he was hurried through school and when he was in primary four he got a double promotion to primary six. Lotanna's mother was always pleased with his efforts and often bought him presents while he was still in primary school. He was eager to succeed and stay ahead in his class. But it seemed such eagerness was abating, giving him over to anxiety and mischief. His mother had become overly expectant, pushing him too hard. Of course, it is not wrong to encourage a child or make him buckle up

to become an excellent student. Yet, what about the danger of excess when some children seem to have as many pressures as harried adults?

Without a thought on the emotional damage such might cause, Lotanna's mother like many parents, felt it was normal to drum into their children's head that winning was everything.

As soon as Lotanna got home on the day he had collected his result, his mother had asked him to bring his result. When he gave his mother his result, fear gripped him, leaving him shaking like a dry leaf tossed by a Harmattan wind. A moment or two later, his mother lifted her head that she had buried in the result she was holding and asked:

"Who came first in your class?"

"It's one boy. His name is Achebe," Lotanna said.

"How many heads does he have, ehn?"

Lotanna had hesitated, looking at his mother as if she had asked a question on rocket science.

"Are you not the one that I'm talking to, or have you suddenly gone deaf?"

"One," he replied.

Lotanna's mother levelled her right hand in the air with her palm wide open. "Just imagine! I thought you would say he has two heads then I will understand why he came first. I see that you're no longer serious with your studies. I made sure you went to the best primary school around. What else do I expect from you if not to stay on top in your class?" For some time, Lotanna wondered if parents of students who were nowhere between first and tenth positions had killed them already since first position was overrated and why it was not honourable to be second in a class of fifty students. How would she even believe that I had tried so hard to come first but to no avail? Why can't I be praised and encouraged to do better next time instead of being bashed? He thought to himself.

"But I did my best to come first, Mom," Lotanna said, feeling dispirited.

"And your best wasn't enough!" yelled his mother. "You used to come first when you were in primary school, or have you forgotten?"

"This is a secondary school, Mom. It's more difficult than primary school and the students came from different primary schools, too."

"So? How many of them finished from De-Citadel of Faith Primary School as you?" asked his mother.

"Three!" he said perfunctorily.

"Is the boy you said came first among them?" asked Lotanna's mother.

"No, he finished from Ozara Primary School."

"Ozara?" she asked.

"Yes. And what about that?" Lotanna was curious. His mother told him that Ozara means bush in Igbo and that it was a shame he allowed a boy from a bush school like Achebe or whatever he said his name was to beat him in class. Thus, Lotanna had spent his Christmas holiday brooding over his mother's harrying demand and criticism.

In school, Lotanna saw Achebe as a stumbling block to his pride of place. If not so, his mother would not have scolded him as though he had gone against a rule or treated something too sacred with scorn. He always did mischievous things to frustrate Achebe and bend his will. One morning after assembly, the Agricultural Science teacher walked into their class and demanded that the students submit the project he had given them to do during the Christmas holiday. The students were asked to look for fifty different flowers, pluck off a small size of each and gum them to a sketch pad they were to buy for it, writing both their English and Botanical names below each. Achebe did a commendable work and brought it to school on the submission day. He placed it under his desk that morning and was conscious of the fact that he did, and rushed out to the assembly with other students, obeying the bell.

Suddenly, Lotanna left the assembly under the pretense that he needed to use the toilet. He walked towards the direction of the toilet through JSS 2 block and slunk into his class when he was sure that no mortal eye was seeing him. He walked straight to Achebe's desk and grabbed his project and mutilated it before joining others on the assembly. When the students were dismissed from the assembly and went into their classes, the teacher instructed them to submit their holiday project.

"Let the class prefect bring them to the staff room," he said and left the class. Achebe was shocked to see that the project he had left in good condition before leaving for the assembly had been destroyed beyond recognition. He wept bitterly and went to the staff room to report that his project had been badly damaged by an unknown person. Mr. Muturu, their Agricultural Science teacher, was not pleased with such complaint; he went with Achebe to his class. Achebe's class was full of the noise from students who were surprised that such had happened. But there was graveyard silence when Mr. Muturu returned with Achebe. He was a lanky man and walked as though he would be blown away by breeze. He was very strict in instilling discipline and the students feared him that they never risked flouting his orders.

"Who amongst you tore Achebe's project?" asked Mr. Muturu. For a few seconds, the students stared quizzically at each other. A look that showed they were plagued with confusion.

"We don't know sir," chorused the majority of the class.

"Don't dare give me that general answer. You can only be sure of yourself not others," he said, his voice was threatening.

"I don't know sir." came their voices. They had refrained from using the "we" to "I," speaking individually. But Lotanna's voice was firmer and louder in defense of himself.

"So none of you had done this, right?" he asked, pointing at Achebe's mutilated project he held close to his chest like a notice board. "Does it mean that there's a book eating spirit in your class, huh?"

The class was silent. Shortly, Lotanna indicated that he wanted to say something.

"Yes, go ahead," said Mr. Muturu. He rose from his desk and said: "I think Achebe is fond of keeping his things anyhow," said Lotanna.

"But I kept it under my desk," Achebe cut in.

"That's not an answer to my question, Lotanna. Anyway, whoever has done this wicked act should know that there's a sad consequence for wickedness. Mind you that anytime I get this kind of report again from your class, I will have no other option but to punish all of you," said Mr. Muturu.

In the end, he told Achebe that he should be more careful with his things some other time; he said his carelessness had caused him the project he had diligently done. "I'm giving you one week to redo your project and submit," he told Achebe.

Achebe was surprised at the teacher's generosity. Rather than punishing him for what he called his 'carelessness', he had given him another chance to redo his project as well as enough time. He put his face on his desk and wept silently.

Chapter Eleven: The Announcement

At about 11 a.m., the following day, an emergency bell was rung to summon the students. The school time-keeper, it seemed, had put a renewed enthusiasm into his job. The principal, a man of average height with a protruding belly and specks of gray on his tangled beard, was already standing on the elevated podium, waiting for the students. The students, especially the new intakes, were surprised to see that it was the principal who had summoned them as they trooped out. Like a big masquerade, he rarely made appearances on the assembly unless there was a need, so many students had begun to wonder what the summon was all about.

"Could it be that Mr. Muturu has reported the issue to the principal?" Achebe asked Lawal, as the duo walked to the assembly ground.

"But if it was so, does he need to call out the whole school?" quizzed Lawal.

"Maybe Kelvin has committed another crime again. His rebellious acts call for great concern." It was Akpan, Kelvin's classmate, speaking to another in a low voice.

When the students had all gathered on the assembly, the principal said a few words about the extracurricular activities, how they encourage students' talents and interests, most especially, how the school had been represented in many sporting competitions at both state and national levels. He also remembered his good old days.

"When I was your age," he told the students, "I was a good footballer and as such I represented my school in football competitions. We participated in the Principals' Cup and twice our team progressed to the finals and won the cup."

The students were drawn in by the principal's narrative and they listened with undivided attention. Finally, he was glad to announce to them that there would be an inaugural edition of the Lagos State Secondary School Relays and would want the school to participate. He told them that the competition was one month away.

This announcement threw most of the students into jubilation. Achebe was so excited that he could not contain himself. He leapt into the air like a leopard in front of the assembly where, according to his height, he always stood. Achebe's over excitement amazed everyone, even the principal, too.

"I see great talents among you: students who will not only make the school proud but will also become great names in the world of sports that will bring fame and honour to our dear nation. It all begins from here," said the principal.

In the end, the principal said that those who wished to represent the school should see Mr. Olatunji Peter later. Mr. Peter was the school's game master as well as the Physical and Health Education teacher. He was a big fan of sports and was always eager to train his students; and they often were neck to neck with their opponents in any competition.

Hardly had the principal descended from the podium and gone back to his office when a sea of students flooded Mr. Olatunji on the assembly and began to say, "Sir I want to run!" "Sir I want to run!" Achebe too was among the teeming crowd, but he was drowned in it that it was difficult for the teacher to see him. His height was a great disadvantage to him. "Will he be able to notice me? he said to himself. As the stampede increased, Mr. Olatunji struggled to keep his balance from those who had elbowed him in attempts to shield others from overtaking them before he finally said: "Listen all of you! It's not about wanting to run; the real deal is being able to run. I have no issue with many of you flocking around me but I have to choose the few that can truly represent the school. Willingness is one thing but strength is quite another."

As soon as he said that, some students retreated and they began to slip off from him as if he had said anyone who knew he was without sin should cast the first stone. Mr. Olatunji looked at the remaining students and said: "Yes, I have my best runners here who can represent us. Akpan, Eze, Rotimi, Habeeb, Kelvin, and Osas, come this way," he said, pointing to the space at his far right. He carried out another headcount which included girls and told the rest that they would be selected after a rigorous training the following day since they were new and untried. Achebe and Lawal as well as others felt disappointed that they had not been chosen.

The following day was a Wednesday and it was usually the school's sports day. Achebe joined others in the field hoping to be selected to represent the school after a trial. Lotanna and Lawal were the first to be called out to run round the field twice. They only ran once before they fell and were breathing heavily as though they wanted to give up the ghost. Mr. Olatunji felt there was no need to continue with them. He dismissed Achebe as being too short and unfit without trying him out. Although Achebe had protested softly that he should be given a trial like others, yet the teacher stuck to his guns. Disappointed, Achebe walked up to his friend Lawal who had now regained himself from exhaustion and told him that the teacher was not being fair for not giving him an opportunity to run as well. Lotanna heard him when he said this and he laughed and teased him about his size.

"When the sun has not shone on those who stand, how will it shine on those who kneel under them?" he said.

Achebe and Lawal did not understand the meaning of Lotanna's proverb. Achebe was so annoyed that he did not pay attention to what Lotanna had said but Lawal asked him for the meaning of what he had said. Lotanna smiled and said if one was told a proverb and he sought explanation of it, it would mean that the dowry paid on his mother's head was in vain. But Lawal said he forbid such and insisted Lotanna explain what he meant.

"Since you need an explanation for a simple proverb," said Lotanna, "no problem! I'll explain. If we that are tall were not chosen to be part of those who will represent the school in the relays, there's definitely no hope for the short ones."

"What are you now insinuating?" asked Lawal.

"Nothing. I'm only saying that your friend shouldn't be angry that he was not tried since his height automatically disqualifies him," he said, raising the corner of his upper lip slightly.

"See Lotanna, you don't disrespect others unnecessarily, okay? What has Achebe done to you that you chose to mock him? What has his not being chosen got to do with height? Why do you hate him so much? It's all about skill and ability not height otherwise you would have been chosen as well," Lawal slammed.

Achebe's face became hardened and twisted with fury that he felt like seizing Lotanna with his bare hands and tearing him into shreds. But Lawal stood in between the two, restraining him. "If you dare insult me again, you will see the other side of me. Are you mad?" Achebe yelled at Lotanna.

Immediately after Lawal had disengaged them, Lotanna went his separate way calling Achebe a short bush boy. Words, especially when they are demeaning and negative, hurt, and Lotanna's really cut deeper and deeper into Achebe's skin.

Beans Myth

Achebe did not completely give up his dream of representing his school in the inaugural edition of the Lagos State Secondary School Relays. But there wasn't any way he could convince the Game Master that he was fit to represent the school, he thought, if he was not tried. He wanted to spite himself but concluded that that wasn't the best thing to do. At home, he would sit all by himself trying to knit strength into the broken tissues of hurt that Lotanna's words had caused him.

One day at school, Achebe saw a woman who had come to drop her daughter off. They were both tall and big as though they came from a family of giants and were standing at the gate. He wished he was even half as tall as they were. Immediately a thought came into him. When her daughter had gone inside the school, Achebe mustered courage and walked to the woman. He greeted her.

Pleased with his show of courtesy, the woman returned Achebe's greeting with "Good morning, my son." "How're you?" she added. Achebe's face broadened with a smile and he said: "I'm fine, ma." "Please ma," he continued, "What types of food will I be eating so that I can be as tall as your daughter?" To say the woman was shocked at Achebe's question was to say the least. For a few minutes, she remained dumbfounded. She wanted to dismiss the boy's question as embarrassing but thought that it would not in any way promote a positive behaviour, if she did. In the end, she smiled and told Achebe that all she knew was that everyone in her family was tall. "As for food, I'll research on the internet to find out what types of foods can help you grow tall," the woman promised Achebe.

Achebe was very pleased with the woman's promise and thanked her very much. No sooner had the woman left than Lawal approached Achebe. "I saw you talking to that woman. Do you know her?" asked Lawal.

"No, I was only asking her about something," said Achebe. "Something like what?"

"Like the types of foods one can be eating to make him grow taller."

Lawal said Achebe was very funny if that was what he was asking the woman. But Achebe insisted that he was very serious. "If so," said Lawal, "you shouldn't have bothered asking her."

"Why?" asked Achebe.

"I should have told you that myself," said Lawal.

"Really? But you didn't tell me you knew it."

"Because you never asked."

"I thought I was your friend. Do I need to ask you everything?" joked Achebe.

"Haha, are you trying to make me guilty or what? Alright, I know of one that Mama Aliyah, our neighbour, told her friend. I overheard her one day telling her friend to always feed her children with beans if she wanted them to grow tall. And I have heard that many times from people," Lawal said. For a minute or two Achebe wondered if the beans his friend had mentioned was different from the type he had been eating even while in the village.

"But I always eat beans even when I was in the village," said Achebe.

"Maybe you don't always eat the right proportion or dose," said Lawal.

"Does one need a particular dose of beans to grow tall?"

"Yes, just like drug prescription comes in dosage for effective cure," said Lawal.

Achebe shook his head in agreement and decided he would experiment what his friend had said. But how could he even influence the choice of food to be eaten and when to eat what, he thought, now that he was still a minor and a dependant? How would he be able to convince his uncle that he had no appetite for the dish he had provided and insisted he wanted to eat beans for three consecutive times or more without him saying I was becoming unbearable? As he sat deeply contemplating how he would make beans his major diet from then on, Achebe got an idea of what to do. Instead of spending the pocket money his uncle always gave him on snacks, he would patronise food vendors even though he did not like to eat out.

At first Achebe's uncle did not see anything wrong with it when his young nephew had for five days refused to eat any other food except beans. He would return from his shop in the evenings and make a list of what food to be eaten for dinner but Achebe would say he had no appetite for such and insist that he wanted just beans. Sometimes too, he would suggest beans and fried plantain. His uncle who had seen that it was cheaper for him compared to the amount that would be needed to prepare other dishes, would not hesitate to go for Achebe's choice of food for dinner. In school, Achebe had become a regular customer of Iya Ghana, a local food vendor popularly known as Mamaput whose menus included bread, beans and dodo.

Iya Ghana sold food under a medium-sized worn-out canopy erected outside the gate of Sasa Community High School, and her major customers were students from the school. As soon as the bell sounded, signaling that it was break, students would call at her place in a large number, each pressuring to be served first before the other. She would yell at them and say it was first come first served; and whoever could not wait for his turn should go. Students liked her food and therefore, they always endured her impolite attitude as long they would be served. It was rumoured that she used white maggi to prepare her food. A substance that induces sweet and insatiable cravings for more, though it causes stomach upset and swelling or bloating of the abdomen.

One day, Achebe joined the endless queue at Iya Ghana's shop and patiently waited his turn. When he had been served the plate of beans and dodo that he ordered, he hurriedly ate it and scurried back to school. It did not take long before it began! Halfway through a Basic Science class, Achebe interrupted his teacher with a violent bang on the desk, closing his right fist tightly while placing his left hand on his abdomen, twisting his body in excruciating pain. The class was thrown into disorder.

"Uhh! Ahh!" moaned Achebe like a woman in labour.

"Achebe, what's it? Are you okay?" asked the teacher in surprise as he moved close to the discomforted student.

"My tommy, sah!" said Achebe with a great deal of struggle.

"What did you eat during break?" asked the teacher.

"Bea... beans, sah," Achebe stuttered.

Achebe's stomach rumbled and he felt a sudden need to use the latrine. He quickly ran out of the class supporting his buttocks with his hands as if he had something there that he didn't want others to see. This made some of his classmates laugh; and some too, pitied him. While Lotanna was pleased to see Achebe in great discomfort, Lawal was empathic. Some who had had a similar experience as Achebe were making guesses, saying that he might have eaten Iya Ghana's beans. Again, Achebe began to feel that his bowel had not been fully emptied after using the latrine. His temperature rose and he began to feel a pounding headache; blinking in quick succession as though something was clouding his vision. Immediately the attention of the school authority was called and Achebe's uncle was contacted through the telephone. The news soon spread around the school like a dry Harmattan wind and many of those who knew Achebe prayed that he recovers speedily.

Achebe spent three days in the hospital where the doctor confirmed he had eaten a food that contained a large amount of monosodium glutamate, MSG—a white crystalline powder that resembles table salt or sugar often used as a food additive. It is commonly known as white maggi and Achebe's system was intolerant of it. He said it could cause permanent damage to the brain and vision. On the evening of the third day, Achebe was discharged and the doctor advised him to desist from eating road-side food.

When they arrived home that day and after they had their dinner of rice, Achebe's uncle sat him down and said it was good that a child should decide on what he wanted to eat at a time, but he thought his recent addiction for beans was alarming and that had almost caused him his life.

"What we love most in life kills us. Just imagine if you had died because of the white maggi beans you ate from a Mamaput it would have been another story entirely. My enemies will begin to wag their useless tongues telling the whole world that I had used you for money ritual. They have always gossiped that my building a mansion in the village is not ordinary. But thank God you're alive."

Achebe had bent his head downward as he listened to his uncle; remorseful. When he finished talking to him, Achebe told his uncle that he was very sorry for making him go through distress. But he was too ashamed to tell him that his sudden craze for beans was because he had been told by a friend that eating it would make him grow tall. He knew his uncle would say he wasn't proud of his individuality. His uncle had told him that he was unique and should be proud of himself he remembered.

When Achebe went to bed that night, he was harrowed by many thoughts. If really eating beans made one grow tall, he said to himself, at least I had a good dose of it for a few weeks now, why am I not growing tall? Could it be that Lawal had lied to me? Or is it just a myth or what? Or was I too foolish to have believed him? But he is my friend, a very good friend and he believed in me when others didn't. I should be able to trust him if that is the least I can do. As Achebe sank himself into a stream of thoughts, sleep soon hunted him down.

Leaving Adult Things for Adults

When Achebe resumed school a week later, his friends were excited to see him looking hale and hearty. Dapo and Lawal thanked God for Achebe's quick recovery and told him that they had missed him a lot. Achebe too, was glad to see his friends again and he said he would never go there when they had joked about going to eat at Iya Ghana's shop during break. He had sworn to it by wetting his middle finger in his tongue, dipped it in the earth and pointed it upward. His friends convulsed with laughter.

However, Lotanna had walked pass Achebe and his friends without uttering a word to them. Achebe and Lawal had let him go without also saying a word to him. It was Dapo who had called Lotanna and told him it was not nice that he had passed them without, at least, saying hi to Achebe who had, because of ill health, not been in school for some days.

"Even if you can't say hi to us at least say so to Achebe who was away from school because he was sick. It could happen to anybody and we pray ours won't be worse," Dapo said.

"And how's that supposed to be any of my business? If someone was hospitalised for eating bad food, was that not what he asked for? Eat healthy and live healthy. I don't waste my pity on people and you can't force me to greet anybody either, Mr. Advocate," slammed Lotanna as he walked away from them, hissing.

Dapo was utterly shocked at Lotanna's response that he stood with arms akimbo and watched him as he went away. Even though Lawal had found Lotanna's behaviour to be unruly, he kept a cool head. He knew Lotanna was not happy to see that Achebe had been back to school and healthy. He had told Achebe how Lotanna had categorically told Michael, his friend, that he was happy about what happened to him and wished he did not return again to school. Achebe was not surprised to hear that; but what surprised him more was that Lotanna could not at least conceal his hatred for him. Soon, Lawal and Dapo began to fill Achebe in on everything that had happened in his absence but he was more excited to hear that Kelvin and his gang as well as some female students had been expelled from school.

"That heartless bully? You don't mean it! What did they do this time around?" asked Achebe? They asked Achebe if he knew the old examination hall behind Chemistry Lab and he said yes. Lawal and Dapo then proceeded to tell him all that had happened. They told him that the second day when he was absent from school, Kelvin, Femi, and Obinna were caught red-handed by the security man making out with three female students after they had steeped themselves in alcohol. The female students they had mentioned to Achebe were seniors and were Kelvin's classmates.

The security man wanted to be sure that no student was still in school or in any of the classrooms before locking up the school gate. He had gone around and inside the classrooms but found no students. He had barely left the Physics Lab and headed towards the Chemistry Lab when he heard the indistinct clacking of desks amidst low moaning of voices. He quickly but quietly walked into the hall but what he saw left him frozen to the marrow. While Kelvin sat in one corner like a boss exchanging gulps of what was contained in an Eva water plastic with a female student, the two of his friends were engaged in passionate romance with other fellow female students. Seeing that the security man had closed in on them, the students who engaged themselves in the unwholesome act all covered their faces in shame and pleaded with him to keep it a secret. Unfortunately, the security man who had decried their act only gave them a false promise. He quickly picked up the Eva water container and perceived its content. It smelled of alcohol.

"So wuna dey drink alcohol too? I talk am before. No wonder wuna dey always talk to elders very rudely! Why wuna no go disrespect elders and teachers when you cannot leave adult things for adults?" said the gatekeeper, shuddering in utter surprise. He warmed them against the dangers of such acts and chased them out of the school compound. This, they told Achebe, had happened after school that day.

The following day, the school principal sent for Kelvin and the other five fellow students. He paced restlessly in his office, waiting for them and contemplating the right action to take. "Not under my watch will there be a repeat of it!" he interjected. Immediately the sound of the bell put all classes on hold and students ran out of their classrooms to the assembly ground. The principal was boiling with rage as he climbed the podium to address the students.

"It's disheartening that," said the principal, "the bad eggs among you want to drag the good image of the school to the mud and bring shame upon my administration. But I'm not going to allow a repeat of what has happened. Never!"

As the principal told them how Kelvin and his gang were caught making out with the female students after school the previous day, the students began to murmur among themselves. "Jesus!" shouted some students, surprised. Kelvin and other participators had bent their heads downward in shame, wishing the ground could open and swallow them.

"Silence!" bellowed the principal. "Kelvin," he continued, "and his cohorts have attested that many of you especially the senior students indulge yourselves in smoking and drinking of alcohol especially dark stout beer which you usually fill into empty Coca-Cola plastic containers to make one feel they are ordinary Coke or Pepsi and smuggle them into the school. A classic case of no problem without a solution, but how could you even think of such solution whose addiction can ruin the lives and dreams of youngsters?"

"This is deceitful! exclaimed one student who was Kelvin's classmate to another, placing both arms on his head as one does to provide the neck with support. "I suspected it wasn't an ordinary Coke when he unconsciously brought it out of his bag yesterday, seriously looking for something."

The principal looked at the murmuring students and hesitated for a few seconds until the noise died down before he said: "You have always had a field day for too long but today marks the end of it all. We're forced to extract the bad tooth as fast as we can so the good ones won't be affected sooner or later. And this, we're sure, will deter others from experimenting with alcohol, marijuana and sex at an age considered inappropriate and vulnerable. Therefore, Ajibade Kelvin, Owolabi Femi, Chukwunonso Obinna, Ekeh Jennifer, Abdullazeez

Rahimat, and Udoh Blessing, are hereby expelled from the school. Henceforth, they cease being students of Sasa Community High School, and shouldn't be addressed as such. Let this serve as a stern warning to the rest. When the lead toad jumps into a pit, will others not retreat to safety?"

Achebe had listened to his friends with keen interest and shock as they took time out to narrate to him all that had happened in his absence. He had always known Kelvin to be a terrifying bully who was very popular in school as much as he was feared by everyone including the teachers. Students called him Big Kay and he often puffed up with pride whenever they hailed him. How could a young boy whose popularity rang a bell, he said to himself, suffer such a disgraceful end? Though Kelvin had dealt with him on his way to the library one day, yet he felt for him and thought he should have been suspended for some time rather than being expelled.

"The principal should have waited until after the relay competition before expelling him since he had been chosen to represent the school," said Achebe.

"Yeah, that would have been a smart act. But I don't think such an idea ever occurred to him," said Dapo.

"When I asked Mr Olatunji why the school couldn't keep him until after the competition as he was training others on Friday, he said the school has a culture of building mind and character, that it was better to save the students from a negative influence than winning laurels for the school," said Lawal.

As Achebe and his friends stood conversing under the walnut trees, the school bell rang and the students all hastened to the assembly ground. After assembly that morning, Achebe did not engage in any idle talk with anybody. He knew he had missed many classes and had a lot of notes to copy. He wanted to cover the academic ground he had lost to his absence, so he set about updating his notes first.

A Gift

Achebe updated his notes and acquainted himself with the lessons he had missed within a week. Although Lotanna's dislike of him had become an open secret among his friends, he refused to be obsessed by its thought. He knew that what lay ahead of him: maintaining excellent academic results and participating in the inter-school relays competition, were of utmost importance to him and they stood before him like a mountain that he needed an unwavering consistency and an invincible will to get to its summit. But how would he be able to prove himself a good fit to represent the school if he had not been tried? Who would the Game Master choose to replace Kelvin now that he had been expelled? Even though he was an enfant terrible of the school, Kelvin was a skilled runner whom the likes of Rotimi and Eze never saw his back.

The Lagos Secondary School Relays would kick off in a few weeks' time and Achebe had known that his chances of ever representing his school in the competition were slim if he would do nothing to convince the Game Master that he was as good as others if not better. After school, Achebe would sit alone at home and began to ponder what to do. When he had put two and two together, he settled for one thing: a gift. Achebe thought that since Valentine's Day was two days away, gifting the Game Master something nice to commemorate that day would earn him a special place in his heart. He felt a pair of shoes would do the trick. Many times, Achebe had heard some students making demeaning mockery of Mr Olatunji, the game master, calling him Mr. One Shoe because he often wore one pair of shoes repeatedly to school until their soles would begin to wear and bend to one side in protest. He often thought teachers were not paid good salaries that would take care of their needs and ensure a comfortable life despite the sacrifices they make in shaping lives and lighting the way for others. But he had not been able to save enough from his pocket money, he said to himself, to buy him that. There must be a way out! That night when his uncle returned from the shop, Achebe told him that he wanted to discuss something with him.

"I hope no problem," said Achebe's uncle.

"There's no problem, uncle," Achebe said, stroking his hair. "Emm..emm just that we're asked to exchange gifts on Val's Day and I randomly chose a teacher while a student chose me."

"And that will be in three days from now," said Achebe's uncle. "What do you wish to give your teacher on that day?" Achebe's face beamed with excitement for letting him decide what gift he would want to...

"A pair of shoes would be great, uncle."

"Shoe gini? Ochoro ogba oso Abiola ya shoe?" What? Does he want to run Abiola race with shoes? Achebe's uncle said jocularly, alluding to the exodus of Easterners from different parts of the country, to their states of origin following a political tension in the land. Some people say it was a paranoiac move. Although it was characterised by annulment, fear, agitation, imprisonment, and death, the event however, transitioned to democracy. Thus, the declaration of June 12. But Achebe had failed to make the connection. In fact, his uncle's question had left him blank and utterly confused.

"What's Oso Abiola?" he asked, his eyelids quivering.

"Hmmm...you didn't do History in your elementary school, did you?" Achebe's uncle quizzed back, surprised.

"No, we didn't, uncle."

"What...? Is it that History has been scrapped from the curriculum or that there are no teachers to teach it? This might be the biggest tragedy that would befall this country if what you're telling me is by any means true." Seeing that Achebe had been webbed in confusion, he quickly buried the matter, and said, "But we don't know his size."

"I think your size is the same as his," Achebe said tentatively.

"How did you know that? All the same, I will see what I can do." Achebe leapt in excitement when his uncle came back the following day and threw a small white box containing a pair of black shoes at him and said, "That's it." Achebe thanked his uncle a thousand times over. That evening, Achebe picked up a piece of paper and carefully scribbled something on it and sellotaped it to the box.

On the morning of Valentine's Day, Achebe was more than excited to go to school. He did not bother taking his breakfast; he swiftly dressed up after a bath, unzipped his school bag, put the gift he wanted to gift his teacher inside, zipped the bag, and zoomed off, feeling as happy as a clam. The atmosphere reflected the day. Because it was Valentine's Day most of the students were dressed in a touch of red and white, and some had come with gifts for their friends and teachers. When Achebe arrived in school that morning, he did not go straight to his class. He went straight to the staff room. He felt a tremor down his spine as his eyes met with those of his teachers who were curious to know who he was looking for as he stood at the doorway. Trembling, Achebe greeted them and softly beckoned to Mr. Olatunji.

"How're you doing, Achebe?" Mr. Olatunji asked as the two walked a little away from the doorway.

"I'm doing fine, sir," said Achebe.

"Alright. Hope no problem," Mr Olatunji presumed.

"No, sir. Just that I brought something for you," Achebe said, rifling through his school bag for something. "This is for you, sir."

"Wow! What a great surprise!" Mr Olatunji exclaimed, his lips were now oval shape and his eyes widened as he cast them on the piece of paper that had been sellotaped to the gift. It reads:

"Thanks for teaching me all I know today. I would be nothing without you. HAPPY VALENTINE'S DAY, sir."

Mr. Olatunji was gobsmacked. For the first time in a long time, he felt the overwhelming joy of appreciation, that ecstatic joy of being a teacher. "Thanks so much, Achebe. You've always impressed us with your brilliant academic performance. You've proven that coming from a village is no academic weakness. But I never imagined you could be full of surprises, too," he said, hugging him passionately. Then Achebe left to his class, feeling like a great achiever, a winner of some sort.

That day was eventful for Achebe. At break time, he went about frolicking in the field with his friends. Although Achebe never got Valentine's Day gifts from any of his friends, he decided that he would gift himself one so he could have something to show his uncle as the supposed gift from a fellow student. From what he had saved from his pocket money, Achebe bought himself a piece of white singlet on his way home.

The Fight

There was no end in sight for Lotanna's hatred against Achebe. In fact, it grew by the day like an anthill and he could not help but show him how much he disliked to see him even in the open. The following week after the Saint Valentine's Day, Mr. Olatunji asked all the participating students to converge on the field for the final training since the inaugural edition of Lagos State Secondary School Relays was only two days away. Mr. Olatunji wanted to make sure that he had the participating students ready and fit for all field and track events before the D-Day. He had the likes of Akpan, Eze, Rotimi, Habeeb, Osas, (and a few others including females) whom he reposed so much confidence in, yet he felt that the absence of Kelvin had left a deep vacuum in his team that needed to be filled. He had thought if he would ever have a great runner like Kelvin?

"But I told you during our very first training that you can't make my list with the way you passed out on a short trial. So, now what are you doing here again?" Mr. Olatunji asked Lotanna who had also converged with others. "I said only the participants should gather here," he reiterated. While Lotanna hung his head in shame and reluctantly left the pitch, feeling picked on, Achebe had stayed behind, unwilling to go, as if to say he would never let the Game Master be unless he had been blessed by him.

As the participants resumed training first with field events such as Short Put, Discus, Hammer throw, Long Jump etc., Achebe stayed on the sidelines and used the opportunity to do some gentle bodyweight exercises. He stretched, foam rolled, jogged, and anything that helped to draw the Game Master's attention to him. He would jog from one end of the field to another and back. At a point he would tell Mr. Olatunji that he could sprint better if he was tried.

"I don't think you're fit for this, Achebe. But if you want to try, I'll give you the chance to prove yourself," Mr. Olatunji said to Achebe, feeling indebted to him.

When it was time for track events training, Mr. Olatunji asked Achebe to join other participants. Mr. Olatunji was impressed with

Achebe's performance during the training that he felt Achebe was a good replacement for Kelvin. Feeling fulfilled by their performance, Mr. Olatunji brought the practice to an end, and announced that Achebe would be participating in the track events with the rest. This got Achebe so excited that he began to whistle an appreciation tune: "He who does good, receive my praise" in Igbo as he ran to his class at top speed, mindful of nothing. He felt on top of the world and wanted to break the news to Lawal and Dapo who were busy playing scrabble in the class. Because he was too excited, he raced recklessly, and as he negotiated the bend to the staircase leading up to his class, whaaaaa! it happened. The unexpected. Achebe had a headlong collision with Lotanna who was going down the staircase. Thus, they tumbled down the stairs, rolling like a head of palm nut, helpless until they found a fixed point on the hard floor. The loud noise of the collision had attracted their classmates. Then, Achebe rose and began to examine his bruised wrist before Lotanna did. When Lotanna looked and saw that his right elbow was dripping with blood, he swore and cursed like a pagan. He grabbed Achebe firmly by his uniform and began to pull him until it ripped off. Perhaps Lotanna would have let go if it were not Achebe.

"Please leave his uniform alone. See how you've torn his shirt," pleaded Lawal and Dapo as they made efforts to unclasp Lotanna's grip while others stood watching. They seemed to be enjoying the struggle at close quarters.

"I won't leave him. Can't you see how he has injured me?" said Lotanna, combat ready.

"But it was an accident; I didn't see you coming," defended Achebe.

"How would you see me, huh? Who asked you to be running without looking. You blind bat," cursed Lotanna.

Achebe begged Lotanna and told him that it wasn't, in any way, intentional, but he would not hear. Though he felt embarrassed by Lotanna's act, Achebe had decided he was not going to lose his temper. But he found himself losing it when, amid efforts to arbitrate their dispute, Lotanna gripped him again and said he would not let him go like that after they had been separated.

"My gentleness doesn't mean cowardice, Lotanna. Just let me go," said Achebe, warning him.

"Do your worst," Lotanna blurted out.

Just then it happened as a flash. Raising his head to look at Lotanna who was way taller than he, Achebe planted his feet firmly on the ground, bound Lotanna's legs with his hands and lifted him above the ground. Lotanna fell with an eruptive quake, unable to rise and fight back. This threw the onlookers in wild jubilation that disturbed the peace of the whole school. Everywhere was in commotion.

"At least this will teach you to stay away from trouble," Achebe told Lotanna as the latter sprawled helplessly on the ground. Even though Achebe felt like a heavyweight champion, he knew his action was unbecoming. During morning assembly the following day, the principal called out Achebe and Lotanna. The principal was full of anger as he stood before the students and spoke to them. He had pulled off his pair of glasses and his face contorted.

"Yesterday, the students you see before you," he said, pointing at Achebe and Lotanna, "decided to throw caution to the wind and engaged themselves in a serious fight thereby breaking the peace of the whole school. Who among you here, if I may ask, does not know that fighting is a serious offence against the school and thus, attracts suspension as may deem necessary by the school authority?" The principal paused briefly to see if there was any of the students who was ignorant of such a rule. But he was pleased that none of them raised his or her hand. "Discipline is one of our core values and we would never for any reason whatsoever compromise that," he continued. "You must know that the school frowns at your shameless display and to deter others from following suit, we've therefore decided that you go on two weeks' suspension. At the expiration of your suspension, you must come to school with your parents." The two were asked to go home with immediate effect.

Achebe's Dream

It was a moment of despair for Achebe. He felt his life was slipping away from his fingers. Alone, he sat at home all day and began to think about the gap his two weeks' suspension would create in his academics—the classes he would miss and his fate of not going to participate in the relays despite his determined effort. He leaned backward on a honey-coloured armchair, creating disjointed beats by tapping his feet on the hard floor, trying to break away from the grip of misery that had enveloped him.

"Tomorrow is the day of the competition and I was suspended from school today after I had tried all means to convince Mr. Olatunji to choose me?" Achebe said to himself, half-statement, half-question. "Oh God! Why nah? This shouldn't have happened now. No...no, I must do something." Just a second later another thought took hold of Achebe, allowing him no moment of peace. His uncle. He thought about how his uncle would feel on hearing that he had been suspended from school for what he could have avoided. "Fighting is for the weak," his uncle would say. "You don't fight to prove how powerful you're. The real power lies in your ability to govern your anger at all times." He remembered the proverb his mother used to say whenever she wanted to deal squarely with any issue for good: If you don't disgrace the rashes at the back, they will not disappear. Should he not have fought? But he needed to disgrace the rashes once and for all. Achebe was caught at a crossroad between two philosophical ideologies—his uncle's and his mother's. "No! I won't tell him. He would be disappointed," Achebe said, shaking his head. Then he quickly gathered his uniform that had been torn in shreds and put them in his school bag so his uncle would not see them.

It was already nightfall. Because he was overwhelmed by an array of disturbing thoughts, Achebe had hardly remembered that he had not eaten anything since morning. After all, food was the least of his problems. Gradually he fell into a deep slumber. It was not a peaceful sleep for Achebe by all indications. Soon, he began to dream but the dream was a frightening and distressing one. In the awful dream, he saw himself at Amasiri with his friend Ugonna and other peers in an "Obu"—a small building where young male folks who are yet to undergo isiji, a rite of passage into the esoteric knowledge of their community—stay at night to thrill Okpaa-abali with songs. They had locked themselves up in the obu to prevent Okpaa-abali—a masquerade whose mystical chant instills fear and terror in the non-initiates—from gaining entry. It is a taboo for the non-initiates to see Okpaa-abali during such appearance and anyone who did, whether inadvertently or otherwise, would be initiated into the Ogo cult at that instant.

Due to the fact that they will be set apart from their loved ones for seven market days during which they will be subjected to a strict discipline, secluded from the concern of everyday life until bravery, toughness and independence become their second nature, no teen would want to see Okpaa-abali much less having a close contact with it. The masquerade had come to them at night to demand some gift items such as groundnuts, oranges, cigarettes and yams from the non-initiates. Achebe and other inmates would sing and entertain the masquerade thus:

Okpaa eh ho oh—oh dreadful masquerade

Bia elegi ji ndeberi gi n'obu ho oh—come see the yam I kept for you in obu

The okpaa would dance merrily round the building to their mellifluous song, waiting for their gift items with bated breath. As they sang for the okpaa, a terrible drama played out. Achebe made towards the door, unbolted it, and slipped off the grip of other inmates as they tried to hold him back from going out in the deep and dangerous night.

"Where do you think you're going? Come back here, okpaa is still outside and it's dangerous," the inmates said, dissuading him. But Achebe would not listen. His mind was made up. He overcame his fears because he wanted to be elevated from the status of ena—a derogatory term for the non-initiates, to a member of an exclusive position in his community at large. He could not wait for his father to decide when; he had to take the bull by the horns.

"Let me go," said Achebe. "Is it not more honourable to die a brave man than remain a weakling under the warmth of loved ones?"

As soon as Achebe ran out of the obu, he was seized by okpaa and carried to ogo—a village square—where, upon arrival, he would meet a group of elders whose spiritual duties were to link him to the spirit world. He wanted to see where his will, courage, and determination could lead him. But unfortunately for Achebe, he was jolted out of his dream when he felt hard and repeated taps on his legs. It was his uncle. His dream had been truncated and his face contorted with displeasure.

"Do you know since when I came back and have been trying to wake you? This one that you're sleeping as if you carried a coffin that was meant for six pallbearers. Hope you're okay." Achebe stretched his body until his joints produced a pop sound before he muttered a good evening to his uncle.

"How was school today?"

"It was fine."

As his uncle made straight for the kitchen, Achebe sat back for a few minutes and began to make efforts to recollect his dream, but only disjointed and broken parts came through.

Achebe Meets Segun

The D-Day was on a Thursday. Because it is environmental sanitation day in Lagos and no shop or company opens till it's 10 a.m., Achebe's uncle did not leave early to his shop that day. On other days, he usually would leave to his shop while Achebe would yet be home preparing for school. Achebe knew that if he stayed at home his uncle would want to know why he was still at home at an unusual time. He did not want his uncle to know that he had been suspended from school for two weeks because he fought. He knew his uncle would be greatly displeased with him. But was he not required to report to school with his uncle at the expiration of his suspension?

While his uncle was still sleeping that morning, Achebe quickly had his bath, rushed his breakfast of jollof rice, and scurried away from home in mufti with his school bag. At first Achebe had no place to go to in particular. He gallivanted from one street to another; then he thought that his friend Lawal would still be at home. Achebe wanted to borrow some notes from Lawal so he could copy them at home when his uncle would have gone to the shop. As soon as he got to Thompson Street where Lawal lived, Achebe ran into Segun. Segun was a senior in Sasa Community High School. Even though he would move in the company of Kelvin and his cohorts, he was obviously a sharp foil. He was compassionate and never bullied his juniors. In truth, he was kind towards them and they like him.

"Good morning, senior," greeted Achebe.
"Morning, Achebe. How are you doing?" said Segun with a broad smile.
"I'm fine. Thank you."
"You're welcome. But where are you going?"
"I want to see Lawal."
"I think I saw him and Akpan in school this morning. They were actually in the midst of other students who stood by, watching the

participants as they were entering a bus that would convey them to the venue for the competition."

Achebe was very surprised to hear that Lawal was already in school. Although Lawal was not an early riser, he had risen earlier that day and had beaten Achebe to the punch. Once again, Achebe began to wish that he would have been among the participants as well had he not been suspended from school. He told Segun that his suspension had deprived him the opportunity of going to represent the school at the competition.

"But you could have asked Mr. Olatunji yesterday if you could still come for the relays despite the suspension," said Segun.

"You're right, but the principal said we must leave the school with immediate effect. In fact, it only occurred to me that I could have asked when I got home," said Achebe.

"And they must have gone by now so they could beat the traffic and of course Teslim Balogun Stadium is a great distance from here," said Segun.

"Yeah, Lawal said so, too. He said going to Teslim Balogun Stadium from here is like travelling from Africa to Europe," said Achebe. Segun laughed so hard and said Lawal's description was an overstatement.

"But he was serious about it," said Achebe.

"He might be right though. Maybe you would like to go with us so you can see for yourself," Segun said suggestively.

"Are you going there now?" Achebe's brow twisted with instant curiosity.

"Yeah, I'm going to meet some of my classmates so we could go together. But on our own arrangement not the school's," Segun pointed out. "Because the school," he added, "provided a bus for the participants only. As we speak, some students too have gone on their own to watch the relays and to cheer our participants up."

"I wish I could go with you guys, but the thing is that I don't have any money with me for my fare," confessed Achebe.

Achebe was excited when Segun agreed to pay his fare to Teslim Balogun Stadium popularly known as Teslim Balogun Stadium, where the Lagos State Secondary School Relays would take place. He thanked him and left off with him immediately.

A Leap of Faith

When Achebe and Segun as well as other students got to Dopemu expressway, they stood for a few minutes and waited for a direct bus that plied Oshodi so they could board another heading towards Surulere from there. As a group, they wanted to board the same bus and get to the venue at the same time. A few buses pulled over for them, but they looked through the remaining space and quickly dismissed them with waves of the hand for want of seats.

"Let's go through Yaba. Surulere is shorter from there," one of the students suggested.

"Why can't we follow Oshodi, and then board a bus going to Ojuelegba. Surulere is just a stone's throw from there. How long do we have to wait for Yaba bus? Besides, the few buses that have passed calling 'Yaba' didn't have enough space to take us all," protested another.

While they deliberated on the route to follow, Achebe stood and merely waited for their final resolution. "Maybe we should go through Oshodi because the more we stand here waiting for a bus going to Yaba, the more we're wasting time. At least we should be at Teslim Balogun Stadium in the next one hour. The event will start at 10 a.m. This is 7:45 a.m. already," said Segun, looking at his wrist watch.

Soon, a mammoth yellow bus popularly known as molue made a stop and its conductor, a lean-faced man who seemed to be bubbling with a lot of energy, hopped out like a monkey and began to shout OSHODI, including names of places the bus was intended to go through to prospective passengers. As soon as the driver brought the bus to a stop, he added, "Abeg enter with your change ooh," giving way to Achebe and others as they struggled their way onto the densely crowded bus through a narrow passage, shoulder-brushing other aggressive passengers who would stop at nothing to rain curses on their offenders. Some of the passengers wore long faces, hardened frowns as if the crumbling weight of the world rested on their shoulders; some too, wore friendly dispositions and would never exchange their humane nature for the beastly.

    The bus crawled out afterwards with passengers standing along the central aisle and the space leading to the exits because the available seats had been occupied. It was not only Achebe's first time of entering such a bus but also his first time of leaving his suburb to another ever since he came to Lagos. While Segun as well as two other students were able to secure seats for themselves, Achebe and the rest stood like prisoners in Black Maria. He had never seen where a passenger would board a bus and still pay a fare for standing throughout the journey. Even though that did not make much sense to Achebe, yet it's a reality in this West Africa's most beautiful city whose population is both a blessing and a curse. As he stood, he began to shudder at the peremptory tone of the conductor as he went round, collecting his money. Though he was happy that at least he could go to Teslim Balogun Stadium, and like others too, he would live to tell his experience. As the bus moved at a moderate speed, Achebe began to imagine that they would get to the venue of the competition in good time and he would be able to participate in the games. But his experience on the way left a lot to be desired that he almost gave up.

    Hardly had they gone passed Ikeja bus terminal and made towards Shogunle when their driver queued behind other fleet of cars that had been caught up in a traffic. Traffic congestion on Lagos roads is a never-ending tale that chokes millions of commuters with frustration as they would spend many hours in a journey shorter than fifty kilometres although some Lagosians humoured it also plays a security role in the city. The reason being that if one is kidnapped in a broad daylight and the police do not intercept your kidnappers, traffic will, they said.

    Hot blood pulsed through Achebe's veins when he realised they had spent two hours or so in the traffic and yet had not reached Oshodi. He became apprehensive about his chances of taking part in the relays. Oh my goodness! Why is this hold up taking too long than necessary? Why today of all days? he said to himself. Meanwhile Achebe would try to squat for a few minutes or even sit completely on the sandy floor of the bus when his legs began to numb from standing for too long. At a point, Segun felt pity for Achebe and vacated his seat for him. Segun's show of empathy was a great relief for Achebe in the course of the journey. When the car that broke down and clogged up the road with traffic was towed, Achebe and his companions got to Oshodi within a short time. But little did they know that the worse lay patiently ahead, awaiting them.

It did not take Achebe and his companions any time to board a bus that plied Ojuelegba via Mushin when they got to Oshodi owing to the bustling activities of commercial buses there. They had been told that it would be difficult for them to find a direct bus to Surulere. Of course Ojuelegba would be their next to last suburb before Surulere. The first few minutes of their journey to Ojuelegba was smooth and the roads were unclogged with traffic. But it happened a little later than they thought. When they had approached the heart of Mushin, the driver as well as the passengers on board saw that people were running helter-skelter and motorists, too, were speeding recklessly in different directions. Everywhere was in great danger. Then the driver stuck his head out of the bus and looked forward to see what was amiss.

"Armed robbers dem dey front! Armed robbers dem dey front!" came a sudden voice from the left lane. It was the driver of an empty bus, flagging down other motorists heading towards the robbery den as he picked up speed towards Oshodi.

Every occupant of the bus froze with fear. Achebe tried to pray silently but was overwhelmed by terror. His heart was pounding heavily as when one crushes a substance into a fine paste using a mortar and pestle. Quickly, the driver stuck his head back in again, parked by the road, turned off his ignition, and waited for the next signal. And it came so soon! Gunfire was heard sporadically, leaving everyone with their hearts in their mouths. The robbery which went unhindered initially had been strained with the presence of men of the Nigerian Police Force. A commercial bank which was not-too-far from the major road was their target. The exchange of gunshots between the robbers and the police was like a clash of two world powers.

As bullets flew in a ricocheting manner leaving scores of people dead, the driver with the passengers deserted the bus in the blink of an eye and ran as fast as their legs would carry them. None cared to wait for the other and none knew the direction he was running to yet they kept running for dear life without looking back. After fifteen minutes of running, Achebe fell over and began to gasp for air. He looked around but saw no one running after him not even Segun who had made it possible for him to travel with the group so that he might participate in the competition. His anxiety grew like mpku—a mound of earth. Where am I? How did I even come this far? How would I find others? How would I get to my destination if I missed them? Achebe thought to himself, troubled.

Soon he rose from the ground, dusted his shorts and his elbows, and began to pace up and down until he came to a narrow road less trod by people. Achebe followed it, meandering through streets yet he was unable to pick his way back to where he had started running from. When he got to a place where there were lots of people who went about their businesses as though nothing had happened, Achebe realised that he had strayed far away; he was some miles away from the robbery scene with no hope of ever finding his traveling companions. Achebe's dream began to sink like a stone cast into a river before his very eyes. He stood for a moment and began to think of what to do. Then he remembered his primary six teacher's favorite saying. Each time he finished teaching them he would say, "Remember that he who asks question does not get lost,' prompting them to ask questions. Achebe decided that he would ask questions on how he would get to Teslim Balogun Stadium. But I have no money with me to continue the journey, he thought.

Achebe walked up to a man in forest green agbada who he believed was old enough to be his father. The man wanted to cross the road to the other side when he saw a little boy beside him looking worried. "Good morning, sir," said Achebe. "Morning," said the man casually as he dipped both hands into his side pockets, waiting for the road to be free of all traffic before crossing; barely looking at Achebe. But that did not deter him.

"I'm going to Teslim Balogun Stadium sir, and I don't know my way."

"Ahh! That's in Surulere," he said.

"Yes, sir," said Achebe, confident that the man knew his destination.

"You have to walk straight down to where you are seeing those yellow buses," he said, pointing to the direction. "You'll see the ones that are going to Surulere."

"Okay sir, but like how much will be the fare?"

"I wouldn't know because I'm not a bus driver. Maybe a hundred naira or so." Achebe thought the man was kind and wished the man knew he had no bus fare. However, he thanked him and walked towards the direction the man had pointed.

As Achebe walked along, he began to think about how he was going to get a bus fare to Surulere. He wanted to go to the bus driver to tell him that he was going to Surulere but had no fare with him. Yet he felt that the driver would be mad at him or might even ignore his plea so he dismissed the thought immediately. Achebe went a little further when he saw a haggard-looking child beggar who softly yet persistently tugged at every passer-by for some money. Many had ignored him and went their way, resisting his grip. But he was amazed at the kindness of some Nigerians who did not hesitate to dole out money to him. I didn't even think of this, he said to himself. Hence, Achebe took a huge leap of faith. He quickly walked past where the man had directed him to board a bus going to Surulere and made towards the bridge, he went because he saw a crowd under the bridge. When he got there, he stood for a moment or two, surveying the environment. Most of the people he saw seemed to be in a mad rush over what he had no knowledge about. Those who stood stock-still were waiting for buses that plied their routes. Gazing pitifully at a young man in a black suit and a pair of glasses that would not stay on well because the right earpiece had been broken, Achebe went to him and said, his lips trembling like a dry leaf, "Good morning, sir. I lost the money for my bus fare; please, help me." Because he had met many of Achebe's type who would come in the same guise, the young man had decided he would not fall for such dubious stories anymore.

He adjusted his glasses as he gave Achebe a leery look. "Ehn-heh, weytin come concern agbero wit overload? Go find your money where you lost am. Abeg carri your cock and bull story dey go front."

Achebe felt dispirited by the young man's unkind words and left; he had to move on although his legs had become too tired and reluctant to carry him. After he had accosted four other strangers and requested their assistance, telling them that he had lost the money his mother used to send him on an errand, and nothing came out, Achebe decided he would try one last time before he would finally give up. Soon, Achebe met a middle-aged man who was drawn in by his story and he gave him a small sum of fifty naira. He had told him that was all he could part with at the moment. Achebe's became a bit cheerful and he thanked the man. He was encouraged by the man's little act of kindness. Shortly after, he ran into another stranger. She was dressed in a mantle adorned with golden details and tassels that hung over her face as those worn by Arab women and headed towards a grey Lexus car. Achebe was guided by a strong intuition to run to her, and he did. He greeted her with an imploring look before telling her that he had lost his mother's money and was in a big trouble.

"How much is it?" asked the stranger.

Achebe's eyes widened. "Five hundred naira, ma."

The woman drew open the wine leather purse she held in her hand, brought out one thousand naira, and gave it to Achebe. "You can go with this." Achebe was lost for words and did not know how well to thank her. He stood waving both hands wordlessly at her until her car was no longer in sight.

Achebe ended his begging spree and hurried to the bus park as soon as possible. Amidst the babel of calls of different destinations by bus conductors, Achebe went straight to the bus whose conductor was calling "Surulere." As he sat on the bus like a boss, he began to mull over the whereabouts of Segun and others. He prayed for their safety, but soon he thought about how he had lied to strangers in order to get a bus fare from them. He wanted to be weighed down by guilt yet he remembered Lawal's favorite quote: the end justifies the means, and became happy with himself. Lawal had told Achebe that his father who was a politician often said it whenever he was with his colleagues. One day, he asked his father for the meaning, and he said that wrong or unfair methods might be used if the overall goal was good. For once during the course of the journey, Achebe's worries, his anxieties, and his hopelessness began to taper off.

The Games

When Achebe got to Surulere, he confirmed, just as he was told, that the suburb was a quiet, peaceful place, and indeed the home of Nigeria creativity being that the National Arts Theatre and National Stadium were planted here. As soon as he had made his way into the stadium, he was marvelled by the sea of spectators who were already seated, waiting for the event which had drawn many schools from different parts of the state. Achebe saw that though he had suffered setbacks on his way, the event was just about to start. He began to snake his way through the stands when he felt a brittle pat on his right shoulder. It was Segun.

"My goodness! Where did you run to? How were you able to get here? We were looking everywhere for you when the shoot-out ceased. Because of that, we missed the bus we boarded; the driver got fed up and left without other passengers, having waited for us," said Segun, feeling excited.

As he turned around, Achebe was pleased to see other companions who could not hide their excitement at seeing that he was able to make it to the stadium despite their fears. "Where's Mr. Olatunji?" Achebe asked. "See him over there," Segun said, pointing him in the direction of the coach. Mr. Olatunji could hardly believe his eyes when he saw Achebe hurrying towards him. "What a pleasant surprise! Indeed you're the son of your father. I was just thinking of you, how your absence was going to affect my team."

After the chairman of the Lagos State Sports Commission had given his opening remarks, disclosing that relays would be a permanent feature on the state's calendar and need to have young athletes who would represent the country internationally, the games commenced at 10:30 a.m. prompt. It started with field events such as Shotput, Long Jump, Discus, Hammer Throw, etc., among the competing schools. Each school wanted to be crowned with laurels so they engaged themselves in a fierce struggle for honours. Surulere Grammar School and De-Citadel of Faith College, it seemed, were in battle of silver medals when Abigail, Eze, and Akpan made impressive leaps, placing

Sasa Community High School atop in Shotput, Long Jump, and Discus. Everywhere was agog when the officials called on the sprinters, beginning with Boy's and Girl's 4×100-metre race.

"Remember the rules on passing and receiving the baton," Mr. Olatunji reminded his team of sprinters, pulling the base of his right ear. Then, he added softly, calling each sprinter, "Habeeb, you have a good start and can run the bend and pass well. You will be the first leg." "Okay sir," said Habeeb. "Rotimi, be the second leg. You run well in the straight and possess sufficient speed endurance. Osas who's confident and reliable in receiving and passing the baton, will be the third leg. You will run to deliver it to Achebe."

He tapped Achebe on the shoulder to get his attention. "You're our last leg. You receive the baton well and you're efficient in running straight with a high degree of competitive spirit. Please do not let us down." "Yes, sir!" Achebe said with vigour. He bent over to touch the ground with his right hand, did sign of the cross before rushing off with others to meet the officials. Competing with them were the sprinters from Baptist High School, Great Leaders Academy, De-Citadel of Faith College, Surulere Grammar School, Dorssy High School, and Jehoshua Royal International School.

The sprint race began with the runners in starting blocks. Each runner was on his lane, and was bent over when the official said, "On your marks." The racers focused on the tracks, having their feet planted in the blocks, fingers on the ground behind the starting lines, hands a bit wider than their shoulders' breadth, muscles relaxed. Then, the official added, "Settt!" and they raised their hips slightly above the shoulder level, their feet pushed hard into the blocks, holding their breath and ready to race with ears opened for the bang. Kpaaak! The sprinters exhaled and ran out of the blocks at top speed.

Even though Habeeb was outran by his competitor from De-Citadel of Faith College, he made sure that he was the second racer to their receivers before other runners. He quickly passed on the baton to Rotimi. Rotimi had levelled up with two opponents who had maximised their chances of widening a lead between them and other runners, and with the right precision, handed the baton to Osas. As Osas moved at the same time with his competitors, Achebe who possessed the speed of lightening stood with right arm outstretched behind him, ensuring that his palm was flat facing the passer. There was a mounting anxiety and wild jubilation among the spectators over who would finish ahead of the other competitors. But none could wager that Achebe, the minutest of them all, would.

"Keelechi! Keelechi!! Keelechi!!! hailed the students of Dorssy High School who had come to cheer their team up, jumping.

"Ebuuka! Ebuuka!! Ebuuka!!! shouted those from Surulere Grammar School.

De-Citadel Of Faith College students bellowed: "Eliijah! Eliijah!! Eliijah!!!

Then, "Acheebe! Acheebe!! Acheebe!!! rent the air from another quarters as the quartets took the lead while others followed.

Each runner was at top speed, keeping their breathing steady, they pushed harder and raced swifter as the cheer rose from the crowd. As Achebe kept pace with them, fear began to wash over him. "Achebe don't give up! Keep going!" Mr. Olatunji encouraged him. Yes, his coach's words were tongues of energy that came upon him. At this point, Achebe's legs gained momentum and he quickened his pace. He began to sprint as if he had electrodes implanted in his muscles, leaving his opponents trailing by over a metre. Achebe ran the overall fastest time of 41.5s to win the Boy's 4x100-metre race while his competitors from De-Citadel of Faith College and Dorssy High School ran the second and third fastest time of 44.0s and 44.7s respectively. There was wild jubilation among the students and supporters of Sasa Community High School.

Abigail was the fourth leg in the girl's 4x100-metre race, and she ran so fast that she topped her opponents. When it was time for 4x400-metre relays, Achebe was already bubbling with a renewed vigour and stood to represent his school. He maintained his unbeaten run for his school, finishing the race at 3.35.4s, though they came second in the girl's 4x400-metre race. Achebe's efforts in the sprint races paid off. In the end, Sasa Community High School was declared the overall winner of the Lagos State Secondary Schools Relays. Impressed with his stellar performance, Mr. Olatunji told Achebe to come to school the following day before supporters scooped and carried him shoulder-high, with gold medals dangling from his neck. Achebe got home that day before his uncle returned from the shop.

Achebe Laughs the Longest

Achebe became the talk of the town for giving his school a resounding victory. When he got to school the following day, he was received with wild jubilation. Lawal and Dapo were proud of Achebe and they walked with him that morning, squaring up their shoulders. Achebe felt fulfilled and like a superstar. He was enjoying his quick popularity. His teachers praised him and told him that his invincible will had brought honour and fame to the school. During assembly that morning, the principal climbed the podium and his face broadened with gladness. He commended all the students who had represented the school in the relays for their indomitable efforts, then he directed his look at Achebe and said:

"If there has ever been a teen with a strong will and a knack for what he loves, then it is Achebe. His type is rare. None had thought Achebe would be at Teslim Balogun Stadium just to represent the school. But I was amazed at his zeal when Mr. Olatunji called yesterday to inform me that Achebe made it to Teslim Balogun Stadium in order to bring home the laurels, despite that he was suspended from school the day before. How we wanted to reckon without our host!"

The students were all looking at Achebe with admiration as the principal commended him. Achebe became a hero of some sort. Though he was a modest lad, praise overwhelmed him. He paid rapt attention as the principal spoke further.

"It's a thing of joy and honour," the principal continued, "that we won the Inaugural Edition of the Lagos State Secondary School Relays courtesy of Achebe. Thus, I hereby revoke his suspension and have him fully back in school. My message to you all is that you should not quit or be ashamed to show the world your talent even when those around you do not believe in you. Your will to succeed in life will pay off someday."

The principal's words were a nugget and as he descended from the podium, many students began to chew over its wisdom. Achebe was overjoyed that the principal had revoked his two weeks' suspension. He thought of how he had lacked the courage to tell his uncle that he had been suspended from school because he knew his uncle would rebuke him greatly. He had lived with the fear for three days now and it was becoming a great monster that was devouring him. For the first time in three days there'd be a cease-fire between him and this monster—his fear. After further announcements had been made, the students began to march into their various classes as the band continued beating the drums, swinging their hands as hard as they could, intoning;

If you do good kingdom, ooh oh oooh kingdom, ooh oh kingdom is waiting for you. If you do bad, no more kingdom, ooh oh oooh, no more kingdom, ooh oh, no more

kingdom, waiting for you...

Achebe continued to enjoy pride of place in both teachers' and students' hearts yet he never drank from the pool of pride despite that he had become so popular. He lived his normal life and even became busier with his studies than ever before. When Achebe returned home the previous day, he told his uncle how he ran for his school and won many gold medals. His uncle was impressed with his efforts and told him that he wasn't, at any rate, surprised, that he knew his skills would one day make him great and take him to places. Achebe said "amen" to his uncle's prayers and thanked him. But his uncle warned him against ever becoming proud. He told Achebe that pride was a great destroyer and it trailed every achiever as one's shadow.

Two weeks later, after the students had commenced their second term examination, a black Jeep drove into the school compound on a Monday morning. Because students were in exam mood and were seen in groups revising their notes, the school environment was relatively quiet. As the Jeep pulled over under a line of walnut trees where some teachers' cars were packed, two men who were dressed in suits to match their black shoes that had been polished to fine gloss, came out from it and began to make their way to the principal's office, following the direction of the school gatekeeper. None gave a thought to who the men were or raised a stare of curiosity at them since inspectors from ministry of education often came in such form and glory.

"Good morning, sir," the visitors greeted the principal when they got to his office.

"A good morning to you, too," said the principal, closing a copy of Punch Newspaper he had been reading before they came in, to give them his full attention.

"I am Steve Udochukwu," said the first visitor, allowing his colleague to introduce himself as well.

"I am Mohammed Abdulazeez."

"We're from the ministry of Youth and Sports," said Steve Udochukwu.

"You're welcome, gentlemen. You may sit down," said the principal. "I'm Mr. Awwal. What honour do I owe this visit?"

"We bring you a letter from the honourable commissioner, sir," said Steve Udochukwu as he handed him a sealed white envelope he had singled out from the file he was carrying. The principal undid the flap with great care before the men and pulled out its content. It read:

"It would please you to know that, as part of the ministry's goals for organising the Lagos State Secondary Schools Relays—to select the best student athletes who would represent the state in matters of sports, your student, Onuwa Achebe, made our list. Therefore, we are glad to inform you that he is among the sprinters who will represent not only the state but also the country in an international athletic championship game in the United States in less than three months from now..."

The principal's eyes widened and his face shone with joy as he read over and over again. "I'm delighted at the news and the little lad will be so excited to hear this," he said as he saw the men off to where they parked their Jeep. He shook hands with them and bade them a goodbye. The teachers were happy when the principal broke the news to them. The principal waited until the students had finished their exams for that day before summoning them to the assembly. He addressed the students with unusual happiness that surprised them. But none of them could make the right guess.

"I believe you all wrote well enough in your exams today," said the principal.

"Yes, sir!" chorused the students.

"I would like to go straight to the reason why I have summoned all of you this afternoon," he continued, fondling the letter. A grave-like silence overwhelmed the assembly ground and Achebe was straining hard to behold the zabiba or prayer bump on the principal's forehead from where he stood. He was tiptoeing in the midst of taller students as the principal darted his eyes about to be sure he was around.

"Achebe, come forward," he called. All the students turned towards Achebe, wondering what it was that he had done. It was exactly two weeks after the principal had revoked his suspension, the day Lotanna resumed school after his two weeks' suspension. Achebe's heart beat faster and his skin turned pale. "But I can't remember committing any crime," he said to himself, placing his right hand on his chest as though it was about falling off. Achebe walked forward even though his feet had become too heavy to carry him.

"Yes," the principal continued, "I'm very pleased to announce that Achebe has made us proud." Achebe breathed in and exhaled heavily. At least, the principal's words had assured him that he wasn't in the school's bad book. "And he's already on the path to becoming a name in the world of sports. The letter here with me," he raised it for all to see, "is from the honourable commissioner for Youth and Sports saying that Achebe along with some other students has been chosen to represent our dear nation in an international students' athletic championship games that will hold in the US in few weeks' time. I knew this would happen someday but I never expected it this soon. Congratulations, Achebe. There's always a reward for passion and I believe your uncle will be happy to hear this," he said.

There was wild jubilation among the students. Achebe was lost for words, he cupped his mouth with both hands as Lawal and Dapo reached out to embrace him. Lotanna stood with mouth agape. Now, he had risen above his hate and envy against Achebe. The news was too great for him not to bat an eyelid, so he jumped in excitement, joining the crowd that had clustered around Achebe. Achebe knew that he had a strong passion for sprinting yet his invincible will, that which had brought him thus far was stronger. It had begun to reward him in great measure. Achebe did not let the grass grow under his feet. He thought of how happy his uncle would be receiving such news and he began to race home at that instant, with his feet almost touching his head.

About the Author

Amadi Ekwutosilam Njoku

Amadi Ekwutosilam Njoku alias Mazi Emeritus Njoku hails from Amasiri, Afikpo North, Ebonyi State. He's a poet, award-winning novelist, playwright, short story writer, literary essayist, critical analyst, and managing editor at Africa Press Chamber(APC). He has authored five books namely Eraz Literature-in-English(a critical analysis of 2011-2015 WAEC, NECO, and JAMB recommended texts), for Senior Secondary schools, Echoes of Our Voices(a collection of poems recommended for JSS 2 by the Lagos State Government), Odogbu The Warrior And Other Stories(a collection of Short Stories for middle-aged) The Invincible Will (a middle-grade novel), and The Weight of Lies(a novel). He resides in Lagos where he has taught the English Language and Literature-in-English in both private and public schools including many SSCE/UTME coaching centres for over a decade before founding Emerito Academy. He has also lectured on a part-time basis at Interlink Polytechnic, Egbeda Study Centre, where he was Technical English and Business Communication, preceptor. He is an SAT, IELTS, and TOEFL instructor. In 2018, his short story titled: Will You Marry Me? got the highest votes for Moonlight Publishers Short Story Award. In 2021, he was nominated for the

World Teachers Day Award. Many of his poems have appeared in some national and international anthologies and tabloids such as Chinua Achebe Essay/Poetry Anthology, Cameroonian and Nigerian Writers League(CNWL), The Nation, Independent, Saturday's Daily Sun Newspaper—a bi-monthly publication and in Poetry Leaves, US. He is a member of the Association of Nigerian Authors (ANA, Lagos State Chapter), the Society for Book and Magazine Editors of Nigeria (SBMEN), the English Language Teachers Association of Nigeria (ELTAN), and the Society of Children's Books Writers and Illustrators(SCBWI), US. He is the 2022 winner of the ANA Prize for Children's Literature.

www.ingramcontent.com/pod-product-compliance
Lightning Source LLC
LaVergne TN
LVHW041543070526
838199LV00046B/1807